SILENT WAKE

By

Robert Pear

2012 Robert Pearson □ Dead Lullabies

SILENT WAKE

By

Robert Pearson

For my mothers

Dorothy and Jill

And my ever loving wife

Rachael

CHAPTER ONE

Calm, but for the tear in the surface

From the seabird's beak

A fish loses freedom

A meal, too short to suffice

Isaac looked at his reflection in the mirror. His eyes studied the image and concluded that he needed to shave. His grey bristles brushed noisily against the collar of his shirt as he turned his head to inspect his jaw line. He ran his strong callused hand across his chin and said to himself, "Leave it another day." He opened the cabinet to replace the shaving foam, brush and razor. The overhead light shone on the blades' surface and flashed a thin shard of light across the ceiling, then down the wall like a slow lightning bolt. Isaac closed the cabinet door and bared his teeth. They were mainly yellow now and not the bright white of his youth. "A smile to dazzle 'em," he thought. Not anymore.

His grey hair was starting to whiten at his temples and stray strands hung loosely over his forehead. Looking out of the small bathroom window, his grey blue eyes watched keenly for any signs of worsening weather coming in from the north. Earlier radio reports warned of a storm brewing further up the coast line towards Northumberland. Heavy rain was forecast to hit the lighthouse in the early afternoon.

At fifty three years old, Isaac Shepherd lived a life of solitude in the Thornside Lighthouse which lay two hundred metres off the East Coast of England, some five miles south of Bridlington on a large grey and black lump of rock. The proud lighthouse stood watching out towards the treacherous North Sea. A winding coil of metal stairs steadily circled up towards a narrow path, only protected from the elements by more boulders acting as a barrier from the winds and sea. Staring straight up at the enormous lighthouse could make you feel light-headed and could bring on a feeling of vertigo. Its bright red stripe cut through the pure white of the rest of the majestic building. The huge bay in which the lighthouse stood, boasted magnificent tall cliffs. They looked as though they had been dipped in different coloured paints. At the base, a deep rich brown encrusted the multitude of rocks, where white flakes of underlying stone broke through the black seaweed. A little higher up, a wash of pale grey slate left the dirty brown behind and reached up to the bleached white summit of the cliffs.

It was February 1970 and time could go very slowly in the lighthouse as not a lot would happen from day to day. He had to keep himself occupied otherwise the solitary life would have eaten away at him. As it was, he loved his life now. Along with fishing he loved to paint. His dear friend, Peter Ambrose, would fetch him the canvases, paints and brushes he needed from the coastal towns dotted around the east coast. Peter delivered food and supplies to the lighthouse and he and Isaac had become firm friends over the years.

Isaac painted seascapes depicting the changing seasons. The dark tumultuous sky on one picture was broken by a sliver of sunlight forcing its way through the clouds to pinpoint a small ship wrestling with the waves. His style was not that original, he knew, although the rough innocence of his first pieces reflected his passion and interest in the sea. Since he had started painting back in 1963, his skills had improved until he was really happy with most of his attempts. He could not stop returning to certain pieces and sometimes over did the details, although the constant tinkering with the paintings would often weaken the impact of the subject. Over time he had learned to leave them well alone and would repaint the scene entirely from scratch rather than ruin the original.

Many of his pieces were sold by Peter on his visits to the local towns and villages. The number of paintings he had done over the years had stacked up into quite an impressive collection. The ones that didn't make it to the bin, or the walls, or the village markets were stored in the lighthouse. Many boxes of his work were stashed away safely and occasionally traded places with the ones he had framed and used to decorate the walls of his home. In each of the three storeys of the lighthouse, boxes full of paintings were stood next to tables, chairs, his bed and behind much of his furniture. Peter had joked that Isaac should open his own gallery. The aroma of oil paint competed with the smell of the ocean but the battle was only temporary and it never managed to overhaul the salty sea.

He took pride in his work whilst carefully reporting the weather and the waves on the canvases. He would always sign his pieces, even those that didn't make the grade. He would always date the painting on the reverse with the time that he started and finished the painting, just for his own pleasure. He liked to know what he had painted and when, as many of them took on the same subject: the sea. It felt to him as though he was recording the changing seasons for posterity. He would add his name and make notes and comments on how he felt he had done and what he had learned. He felt that this would come in handy someday. So, far it hadn't.

Not all of his paintings focused on the sea. Quite a few of them were of the many seabirds that nested in the great chalk cliffs. Black and white guillemots, gannets and razorbill seabirds would often fly down to the rocks surrounding the lighthouse and feed on the fish that lurked beneath the lighthouse tower. He would love painting these wonderful creatures. The black hood of the razorbill stretched down its back. Just a thin white line would extend out from its eyes to the tip of its black beak. Their inquisitive look at Isaac made him laugh as they tilted their heads over to one side and then the other. "What are you thinking, little bird?" Isaac would often say to them. In answer, they would cock their heads over to the other side, ruffle their feathers then take flight. Isaac would watch them fly back to the cliffs to their families.

Guillemots would occasionally compete with the razorbills. Squawking and flapping, they would fight on the rocks to try and ensure that they got their share of the fish. Their faces were black but would sometimes have a blue hue once the seawater dripped from their feathers. One bird seemed to always find Isaac. He had fed this one from his hand on numerous occasions since it was young. The rip in its left wing always gave him away. Some injury had befallen this little bird while it was very young, but its endurance and spirit touched Isaac's heart. It would walk around the lighthouse to find his friend and would stand waiting patiently at the open door.

The origin of the guillemots name came from the French for William, so Isaac named the little bird Bill. Bill would squawk at Isaac to feed him when he was young. "Good morning Bill," Isaac would say and give him a nod of the head. Isaac brought out his bucket filled with fishing bait. Bill would step from side to side impatiently waiting for his morning feed.

"Head of the queue as ever," Isaac smiled down at the little bird. Bill was the only one in the queue as the other birds liked to keep their distance. He put his hand into the bucket and retrieved a large piece of bait. His pocket knife gleamed in the light as he brought it out of his jacket pocket and sliced the meat into two pieces. "We don't want you to choke on your breakfast, do we?" Bill hopped closer to Isaac with his beak wide open. Isaac tossed the fish to the bird.

"Two pieces today," Isaac said as he flipped the other piece towards his feathered companion. Isaac looked up at the sky. "I think you need to find some shelter. The weather's going to change soon," Isaac said as a gust of wind whistled through the sea air and the waves started to look more fierce. "We're in for a big one this time." Bill looked up at Isaac as if hanging on to his every word although he was more interested in the contents of his bucket rather than the old man's voice. Once he realized that breakfast was over for another day, Bill beat his wings and struggled to get airborne. The tenacious seagull rode the wind and climbed high and back to the relative safety of the cliffs.

"Fly home, Bill," Isaac called after him.

Isaac felt as though nature lived with him at the lighthouse. On some very rare occasions he would be visited by of a couple of puffins. Their large colourful beaks almost made them look tropical compared to their black headed cousins. They weren't as friendly as the other birds and stayed only for a short while when Isaac came outside. He managed to get decent views of them while they fed and had managed to paint some beautiful pictures of them. He would carefully sketch the birds onto the canvas when he had the chance. Filling in the details from memory proved difficult at first but after a while he had managed to recreate some very fine birds on the board sat on its easel. "I should buy myself a camera," he would promise himself. A promise, as yet unfulfilled.

The storm hit the lighthouse that afternoon. The thunderheads had been building all morning from the north as suspected and the rain and wind brought in the big waves. Huge waves broke on the side of the lighthouse and the spray soaked the windows on the second floor. Rain angled in steeply from the ominous black clouds. What sunlight there had been was soon a distant memory. Isaac sat inside the lighthouse, protected from the storm outside. The red and white striped lighthouse stood bravely on the rocks and took each wave as it came. February 1970 was cold. Very much like the previous winters Isaac had known.

Life in the lighthouse had always proved to have been good. His initial days and weeks had seemed to be such a contrast to his previous hectic work life in the navy and later, working in his father-in-law's textile firm. This life was much more suitable for him and he found it aided the healing of his broken heart. His marriage had failed, yet his love for Alice would always be a part of him. In the early days of his life in the lighthouse, the lapping of the ocean on the rocks soothed him although he was lucky to have such calm weather when he started. It soon changed along with the seasons and bad weather struck the lighthouse hard. The east coast had always been a turbulent area for the weather and throughout much of the nineteen sixties it had proved to follow the same pattern as previous decades. The first weather satellite launched in April of 1960 had given people a better understanding of weather fronts and also of what to wear the next day. To Isaac, it made no difference. The weather would do what it needed to do and there was nothing to stop it.

Although, life was good for Isaac, he had recently been hearing strange things. Odd noises had begun to manifest in the mists of the sea. The previous night had been one of the nights.

The fog horn fell silent. The fog seemed to be thicker than normal. Isaac watched the lighthouse light cut through the mist, but it was not making much of an impression. The light was being eaten up by the fog. The quiet was eerie, even for Isaac. The deathly smog-like blanket held secrets deep within and Isaac needed to know what was out there. Knotted swirls of grey swam in front of his eyes. He looked up and saw that the penetrated only a few feet into the thick fog. Suddenly, a faint sound made its way through. Isaac stood still and listened. He could hear music; dance band music. It shifted in and out of earshot as though it had its volume turned up and then down again. It phased through the fog in short waves of aural supremacy over the mute mists. Isaac strained to try and make out where the noise was coming from. The music faded and died. The fog in front of him seemed to darken as though a huge shape was sailing by the lighthouse just feet away from him, moving from right to left. He could hear the water part as if some giant had brought its huge foot through the silent ocean and was wading to the north. He held his breath as it passed. Mist swirled and formed a silent wake behind the phantom. Isaac's heart beat faster and it was now the only sound throbbing through his brain. The fog began to clear and the horn came back to life with a booming blast. Isaac threw his hands over his ears and tightly closed his eyes. When he opened them, the mists had lifted and he could now see the familiar North Sea stretch out to the horizon. He looked over to the north to see if he could discover what had just gone passed. There was nothing. The sea was quiet and empty. He wrapped his coat around him for comfort and stepped back into the lighthouse. What had just happened? His brain had no answer.

It had unsettled him, although he initially put it down to the solitude he experienced. His mind might have conjured up some strange anomaly. Or had it?

Other than the disturbing sounds, he had settled in well and found that it had been an excellent move for him. Fresh sea air everyday lead him to have a wonderful unbroken sleep pattern, something which had been missing for so long. His dreams and nightmares of his wife had plunged him into despair. Her betrayal and her death had affected Isaac deeply but the moving to the lighthouse had eased some of his woes.

However, as the first year moved on to autumn and winter he did find that the boom of the foghorn and the incessant weather made sleep difficult. Makeshift ear plugs did their job in blocking out the noise, but he soon learned that he had to be able to listen in case something out on the ocean went wrong. The plugs were discarded and he became one with his environment. The slightest difference in tone from the wind and he'd notice it. That came with time and he knew if something didn't sound right; the creak of the lighthouse, the sound of the waves striking the rocks and the lighthouse outer wall.

One of the most wonderful things he had noticed was that he would be woken each morning by the numerous birds flocking around his windows. Had no real need for an alarm clock. The seabirds hailed a new morning with their screeching and calling at five o'clock each morning. He'd awake with a satisfying stretch and ready himself for the new day ahead. Bathe, shave (most days) and clean his teeth then down stairs for his breakfast. Black tea or coffee set him up for the day. In spring and summer, he would stand outside the great storm proof door and take in the wonderful sights. With mug in hand, he would walk around the path at the base of the lighthouse marvelling at his good fortune. He enjoyed watching the birds swoop and feed, making their way to the sea and back up to their waiting young in the chalk white cliffs. Bill would be there most days to say "hello". Not all of the cliffs were this pure. Huge black slabs dug deep into the side of the monument of rock and rubble. In the distance, green fields rolled away to the villages and towns. Many of the fields were dotted with grazing cattle, cows and sheep.

Tall cliffs almost five hundred feet high, surrounded the bay encasing the waters within and doing their best to keep the waters more calm than the open sea. Depending on the currents and the time of the year, the waters could be covered in small ripples, whilst the sea just two miles further out to the east were swelling and squalling. Of course, should the winds change and the Gods see fit, then the sea could turn and bring devastating waves into the bay and crash against the lighthouse tower and the shore behind.

Although today's weather would be keeping him on his toes. The wind and rain lashed the side of the lighthouse as Isaac stood on the main gallery looking out to sea. A crack in the clouds allowed the Sun to peep through and battle with the storm. He looked back up at the glass of the lantern room glimmering in the Sun soaked rain, and saw tiny rainbows play across its smooth surface. It was ten o'clock now and even with the rain, the visibility was beginning to improve. He decided to go back inside and switched on the radio.

"Love grows where my Rosemary goes" drifted out of his TR130 Bush radio and filled the watch room as Isaac checked the fuel and food supplies. The lighthouse was made to hold all the provisions it needed, although it was a very cramped space. A quick stock-take and Edison Lighthouse had finished their ode to young Rosemary.

Rolf Harris then piped up telling Isaac all about two little boys, and that wasn't what he wanted to hear. He turned the dial to pick up the Third Programme. He still referred to it as that even though the name had changed to Radio Three almost three years earlier. He quite liked some of the music on the Light Programme, now named Radio Two, and enjoyed listening to their delightful airings. They were still playing reruns of Hancock's Half Hour. The great British comic had taken his own life two years previously, and that saddened Isaac. "Things just seemed to go too wrong too many times" wrote Tony Hancock on his suicide note. "A sad loss, a very sad loss," he said out loud to no-one in particular.

At £5.65, he had always thought the radio had been worth every penny. Not so the television set he had treated himself to. The RCA CTC-16 colour television came in a wooden cabinet and had cost him £120. It sat there sullenly whilst the little Bush radio got all the attention. "There'll be something worth while watching one day," thought Isaac.

Isaac turned the dial of the radio and found the radio playing Haydn's "Farewell" Symphony number 45, which made him smile. As the music filled the room, Isaac walked back out onto the gallery just as the snow started to fall. The wind whipped the white flakes around his face as he wrapped his warm winter overcoat around him and slanted his eyes and looked out to sea. Visibility had started to fade and the sensors on the fog horn begun to kick in. The Sun had retreated behind the clouds and refused to take any more part in the day to come.

A deep bellow broke the silence, and vibrated through Isaac's body. His legs trembled with each blast. As the snow worsened and the sky turned white grey, Isaac stepped back into the relative warmth of the lighthouse. Closing the door, Isaac brushed the snow from his coat. He hung it on the left of the large white door on its designated hook. Three other coats and jackets hung on the right waiting for their turn to be worn. A waterproof wax jacket sat neatly next to the heavy wool coat, with the short gabardine windcheater imported from the United States completing the trio.

The melting snow dripped into the bucket below the hook. Isaac didn't want the whole floor getting wet, so had put the tin bucket there to catch any of the water that would drip from his coat. A shallow pool had begun to form in the bottom of it. Isaac watched it aimlessly. The boom of the fog horn brought him back.

Isaac climbed down the steps to the VHF radio and turned it on. He wanted to speak with George Meade, the captain of the lifeboat which operated out of Bridlington. He tuned it to 158 MHz and spoke into the microphone.

"Thornside Lighthouse calling Alpha, Charlie, Golf, eight, seven, seven. Calling Alpha, Charlie, Golf, eight, seven, seven. Over."

A slight crackle then a short delay. "This is Alpha, Charlie, Golf, eight, seven, seven. Morning Isaac. What's the problem? Over."

"Morning George. We have got some heavy snow coming in and visibility dropping to around two nautical miles. The fog horn has activated. Just wondered if there were any ships out there. Over."

"Our radar is picking up two fishing vessels four nautical miles out and five and a half nautical miles out. Should be fine, Isaac. Over."

"Thanks George. Just wanted to check. Over and out."

The lifeboat, ACG-877 Lizzie, patrolled the East coast from Bridlington down to Withernsea. A total of twenty six nautical miles. The next lifeboat to the north was stationed at Flamborough Head at North Landing. That boat, the BFF-775 Betty Groombridge crew would assist the Lizzie if they were ever called upon.

Isaac clicked off the radio set and looked out of the window. The sea's waves peaked in white froth and mixed with the snow, crashing into the lighthouse walls. The foghorn continued its warning booms. He had only ever spoken to George Meade over the radio, but Isaac's friend, Peter knew him well. Isaac had never met him face to face before. George's six man crew had been patrolling these waters for seven or eight years now, and had been called into action many times. The Sea King helicopter had only just come into service and the Coast Guard liked to make its presence felt. The yellow pride of the Coast Guard worked alongside the RNLI Lifeboat and covered twice the area that the robust boats could cover. Isaac had not spoken directly with the pilot of the helicopter at all, but he had seen it fly by on numerous occasions.

Isaac turned his attention to a full check of the lighthouse. The first aid kits were fully stocked with tablets, gauze, creams, bandages, plasters and all the usual items. The fire extinguishers had been checked two months previously. The whole lighthouse was tidy and safe, all cabling was neatly tucked away and food was stored in its rightful place. Isaac ran a controlled and efficient lighthouse. He didn't know how to do it any other way.

The next morning, Isaac cast his fishing line. The seagulls were having more luck than Isaac that day. They swooped down to pick fish after fish out of the blue green sea. Isaac cast his line and could see that the seagulls had frightened most of the fish away from the lighthouse. It was as if they knew that Isaac was trying to find his lunch and they were going to try and put a stop to it. The fish would have to wait another day. Isaac pondered what roasted seagull would taste like.

As the day drew on, the weather eased and the Sun decided to make another appearance and broke through the grey clouds. Isaac took the chance to check the windows of the lantern room. Stepping out onto the gallery, he scaled the twenty steps up to the landing in front of the windows. He circumnavigated the lighthouse tower, checking for any signs of cracks or damage. Each of the eight windows he passed created its own portrait with a different background. The view behind him changed from the black rocks with grey clouds to snow and a restless sea, to white, chalk cliffs with guillemots and finally to green hills and Sun. Four views showing the four seasons split between the eight windows.

At each of the windows, he stopped and studied his reflection. The first two reflected the rocks with the Sun shining on the right hand side of his face. Two similar views, but with a slightly different slant. He thought it made him look handsome and as rugged as the rocks below. At the next two windows, his white stubble reflected the Sun's rays through the glass and his eyes shone. White, blue and yellow prism light danced across his features. The light seemed to make his wrinkles disappear and the sea and clouds gave a washed out background. He liked that. "Maybe I should have a go at a self portrait" he mused. The next image featured a number of white seabirds swooping out of their nests down into the sea to pick out careless fish as the Sun lit up the left side of his face. He stopped at the final two windows of the hexagonal structure. The hills in the background looked lush and the blue sky's wispy white clouds looked to be beautifully painted on an azure canvas. His face gave no reflection. His dark silhouette seemed like a black hole of nothing. An abyss? What was the saying? "And if you gaze into the abyss, the abyss gazes also into you". He felt a chill run up his spine and up through his neck until his head hurt. The contrast of the bright Sun and the wondrous view was spoilt only by his own reflection. Although, it didn't really look like his reflection at all. His body looked alien to him, something he had never seen before and something he certainly didn't like. Even the shape of his body looked deformed. The shape of his head, even with the waterproof hat fastened tightly, seemed wrong.

He was looking at someone else's reflection!

He unfastened his hat and took it off, then turned his head to the right and tried to look to the left to see if it was his profile. The image did not improve. He stepped closer to the glass and he stared into the eyes of the reflection as it moved shakily toward him. It was him, not some demon or monster. He took a sharp intake and wiped the glass with the cloth as though to extinguish the horror from the surface. Or was it beneath the surface, now embedded within? Isaac blinked a few times and took a deep breath to rid him of what he had just seen and felt better although the image wouldn't leave his thoughts. A shadowy smudge faded from the glass.

As he reached the top of the steps which would take him back to the sanctuary of the watch room, he turned and looked at the lantern. The glass looked as it always had done. He scanned the glass, looking for any imperfections, but he knew there were none. What had he just seen? What did the reflection mean, if anything? Was he losing his mind?

"Stop it" he said aloud, before descending the steps.

Once inside, he made himself a cup of tea. He fetched the whiskey from its usual place, behind the television, slipped a drop into his tea and pulled over his favourite chair. Drinking in a lighthouse was strictly prohibited but Isaac kept a bottle just in case he had received any bad news or had a shock or if he had gone through a really bad day at the office. This had been one of those moments. This had been a shock. He placed the chair in front of the window and looked out to sea. The snow had now stopped and light rain replaced the icy flakes. He couldn't shake the ominous feeling.

It was now half past four and the light had begun to fade. The light from the lighthouse's huge lamp swept across the black water below. Once, twice then a third time. On the third pass it stopped to shine out at sea. Each lighthouse had its own timed flashes to tell passing ships where they were and which lighthouse was lighting the way. The weather had settled, but it was bitterly cold. Isaac turned on the television he had saved up for, and once it had warmed up he turned the dial. "Crossroads" came on, to which the dial was hastily turned again. BBC 1 promised "Jackanory". The children's programme had a different story teller each day. Isaac thought, "Not for me," and the television was turned off again. Why did he actually buy the thing?

Isaac turned on the radio and listened to the soothing classics of Beethoven and Wolfgang Amadeus. As this was playing, he started to prepare some food.

At just before eight thirty, he turned the television on again just in time to watch The Dick Emery Show on BBC 1. He reached for the bottle of whiskey, and poured himself a small large one. At £2.64 a bottle, it was his most extravagant expense. Well worth it though, he thought to himself.

Had he said that out loud? He couldn't tell anymore. Isolation and solitude did that to you.

Or was it just him?

And was he alone?

He settled down in front of the television and laughed at the comedy sketches being played out. His laughter became a little too shrill at times which frightened him. It sounded more like panic.

"Ooh Isaac," said Dick Emery and looked directly out of the screen at him. "You are awful, but I like you". Isaac shuddered and stared at the screen. Had the comedian on the television set just spoken to him? Looking down at an empty glass he knew that it was time for him to go to bed. He tentatively walked over to the television, turned off the set and took his whiskey glass over to the sink and rinsed out the intoxicating remnants. He took a fresh glass down from the cabinet and turned on the cold tap. Ice cold water filled the glass and he took a drink. He turned to look at the inanimate television and then climbed the steps to his room.

That night, he had a restless sleep. His mind meandered through the day's events and the strange and unusual thing that he had seen in the windows. The wind had dropped and the rain subsided, but a storm had entered his thoughts.

Another time, another him stepped through the door of an old lighthouse. The wooden structure twisted and groaned with the wash of the sea. The whole lighthouse tower bent and swayed with the movement but Isaac managed to stay upright. The wet wood squeaked and Isaac could see the ocean beneath the broken floor of the lighthouse. He stepped assuredly across the boards towards the steps which lead to the first floor. The windows were broken and glass lay splintered upon the floor. Smoke filled the first room, but Isaac moved forward undeterred. At the top of the next flight of stairs the smoke became so thick that he couldn't see a thing. Then the thing saw him. The black shape moved quickly towards Isaac through the smoke to reveal itself. It knocked him down and then pinned him to the floor. Its long grey beard smoldered and its eyes were fire red. Smoke tendrils made their way out of those dark demonic eyes and nostrils as it shook its head violently from side to side. Its hair was a blaze of fire and spat sparks across the room, illuminating the dead bodies. Bodies that were stacked around the room in various states of decay. Most were covered in seaweed as crabs and unnamable things scuttled across their black burnt corpses. The heat haze rose around the room giving a bloody red shimmer to the grotesque scene. Dark, deep red smears covered the walls and the pungent smell of death filled Isaac's head. Bodies upon bodies were heaped high around the perimeter of the room as the sparks ignited the dry wooden skeletal structure of the lighthouse. Isaac stared into the face of the creature lying heavily on his body. It screeched and flailed, whipping its flaming hair across Isaac's face. His ears winced at the high pitched scream which came searing out of the black hole of his captors mouth. Isaac tried to shake this monster off, but it grew heavier with each move Isaac made. The talons on the end of its fingers scraped and clawed into his skin slashing and wounding him with callous hatred. The dead bodies began to move slowly, jerking their broken bodies in a hideous dance. Isaac watched them crawl and twist towards him as the fiery demon laughed and cackled. Flames now filled the room with a heat and light so fierce. Isaac took in a deep breath and closed his eyes.

Isaac screamed and sat bolt upright in his bed. It was pitch black but for the dim light coming through the window behind him. He could make out the familiar things in the room. It was his room. The only sound now was the gentle ticking of his clock. It read two-forty.

Sweat dripped from his entire body and stinging tears pricked his eyes as he sat there in fear. His tongue felt as though he had tested a battery on it to see if it was live. Then the panic filled his mind. As his eyes became accustomed to the dark, he stood up and went to the bathroom. He switched on the light and the capacitor in the starter motor flashed briefly and ignited the fluorescent tube. He turned on the cold tap, and buried his head underneath it letting the ice cold water cover his neck. The cool water cascaded down across his face and beard. He turned his head up toward the tap and let the water spill over his lips which he lapped at. Grasping at a towel, he wrapped it around his cold wet head, and rubbed rigorously. Then he took the glass from the cabinet and poured himself some cold water. He looked in the mirror. He saw his face looking back at him. What did he expect to see? A flaming demon with hair and eyes on fire?

"Old fool," he said out loud. Hearing his own voice calmed him a little.

It was quiet in the lighthouse. He looked out of the window and saw the familiar light of the lighthouse flash across the still sea. The calm before the storm, he thought.

He looked at the clock and saw it was a quarter to three in the morning. He put on his trousers and pulled a jumper over his nightshirt. He slipped on his boots and put on his heavy woollen overcoat and headed up to the watch room. He looked around and everything was how it should be. He opened the door to the gallery and stepped out into the moon-lit night. He took a deep breath of the sea air, filled his lungs and breathed out. His head felt heavy and dizzy. He gripped onto the safety rails and looked straight ahead. He didn't feel good. The stars shone beautifully in the night sky and the moon's reflection broke the black ripples upon the ocean's surface. He took another breath, and felt better. He looked across the North Sea and saw a ship in the distance as the light from the lighthouse swept over the scene protecting all in its swathe. He smiled and waved to the ship, but it was about five nautical miles away and would never see him. He knew that but waved anyway. It comforted him that there was someone else out there. He stood there for an hour before taking up the courage to go back to bed. He had to be back up at five sharp, and he needed his sleep. The seagulls would be his alarm. A couple of hours with his head down would be the best for him, as long as he could sleep.

Isaac stepped back into the lighthouse and began to undress. He thought he heard a faint whisper: "Isaac". He walked over to his chest-of-drawers and saw her familiar face looking back at him.

He picked up the photograph of Alice and ran his rough hand over the glass. His fingers smeared the clear surface as he looked down at his wife. She was laughing, smiling at the photographer. A strong gust of wind had caught her hair and tossed her fringe over her pale blue eyes. He recollected how smooth her skin felt and the sweet smell of her breath. It was always fresh as though she had been chewing on a peppermint leaf. Rain began to cover her face and a fresh deluge spilled from Isaac's eyes.

"I miss you."

He got back out of his clothes and slipped between the sheets. He stared up at his ceiling, wiped away his salty tears and slowly closed them. He took three deep breaths and drifted in to sleep.

CHAPTER TWO

Too cold to breath

But no time to stay

To sink or swim

Break the ice away

He saw her coming out of the grocer's shop with her mother. Her hair bounced along as she walked across the street, almost dancing with her joyful movements. Isaac watched as she stepped up onto the curb of the pavement. She was dainty and delicate, maybe seventeen or eighteen, he couldn't tell. The girl looked over at him. At least Isaac believed that she did.

Isaac followed the mother and her daughter across the street and was almost hit by an oncoming car. The car braked heavily as Isaac planted his hands on the warm bonnet. The driver glowered at him and raised two angry fingers as Isaac stepped aside and shot the irate driver a smile and a wave. The young girl stood with her hand over her mouth and eyes wide open. Those beautiful eyes met Isaac's. He froze, although quickly realised that he was still prone to further danger from the cars driving by. He quickly made his way over to the safety of the pavement.

The girl was dragged away by her mother's wilful hand towards their intended destination; the coffee shop.

The bell sang merrily as the door swung open and the two women soon found a seat near the window. A waitress came over and took their order of two cups of coffee, a chocolate cake for the girl and some seed cake for the matriarch. As the waitress left to fetch their order the mother shot a warning glance at Isaac through the window. He smiled in spite of the glaring eyes of the older woman.

"A little too forward," he thought to himself and stuffed his hands deep into his pockets, nodded to the mother and daughter staring out of the café's window and carried on walking down the path. His heart felt as though the young girl had given it a squeeze.

Alice strained her slender neck to watch as her handsome suitor walked away. A slight crease appeared on her brow as she crinkled up her nose as she saw him walk away. Her mother brought her back to reality by coughing loudly several patrons turned around to the embarrassment of both mother and child. Alice shifted in her seat and looked up into her mother's face.

"Yes?" her blue eyes seemed to ask.

"Child!" her mother scorned.

Days went by and Isaac couldn't get the thought of the young girl out of his head. He'd walked past the coffee shop several times everyday over the past two weeks and had not seen her again. He didn't feel as though he was obsessed by her. How could he be? He'd seen her once, had not spoken to her and didn't know her name. Yet, he could not stop thinking about her. He closed his eyes and he could see her shape and could visualise the way that her hair moved. He was obsessed. "Damn!" he spoke allowed.

He sat in his tiny flat overlooking a small park which housed an allotment bordering on the north side. His flat held very few things as he had no need for great splendour. His income from his work as an engineer wouldn't extend to lavish living, so he lived life as simple as possible. He sat on the old chair in the flat; a worn out threadbare seat which offered very little comfort. A table, which looked as though it had barely survived a direct hit from a stray bomb in the Great War, stood mournfully against the wall opposite him. Above that hung a faded painting which declared that the artist was not as talented as he may have thought that he was. A rudimentary landscape of browns and greens muddied the canvas and gave no inspiration at all to the viewer. Other than his single bed, the only other piece of furniture was his chest of drawers which took up almost as much room in his bedroom than the bed itself. It had belonged to his father. The father who he had never met, but Isaac felt a strong affinity with him through the old piece of woodwork.

The cream wooden door led onto the first floor landing of the old Victorian house where he lived. It kept the world out there and his thoughts safely stored in his room. A room much like the other five rooms in the old house. At present, he was the only tenant living there. His landlady left him alone as long as he paid the rent promptly. She was the only one to bother the paintwork on the door with her annoying rapping once a month to collect per payment.

He stood up and looked out across the park. The Sun warmed those who were out for a promenade and ensured that many a handkerchief was used to disperse the sweat from the brows of those unlucky enough to be working in such a heat. Several families idled across the greenery as children played in the shade of the three great oak trees which formed a cluster at the far end of the park. Three giants looming over the scene like a trio of sergeant majors controlling all events and aspects of their small domain. The Sun played through the leaves and dappled the green lush grass below with swaying patterns. The children ran and screamed as they tried to catch the shadows dancing on the grass. Dogs barked and chased their tails with no real luck of catching them.

His body felt a jolt of electricity flow through him and his legs became warm and his hands began to perspire. There she was, walking slowly through the park. A slight breeze played in her hair and she delicately brushed it out of her face. She turned to readjust herself and looked up at the window where Isaac stood motionless. She seemed to turn to stone at his gaze as though he taken on Medusa-like qualities. She smiled and he saw the softness of her features light up the whole park. Isaac watched transfixed at her porcelain features which seemed to crack as her mouth turned up gently and her eyes coquettishly looked down at her gloved hands. Isaac brought his hands up as if to say "Stay there." She seemed to understand and nodded.

Isaac threw on his brown shoes and he fumbled with his laces. "Come on, Isaac" he coaxed. His fingers were failing him and all he could think of was that young woman would lose interest and soon be gone. Was she a phantom or had he really seen her? Could his mind have played a trick on him and manifested his desire in the park opposite? He stumbled, bent in two still trying to tie his shoe laces and staggered towards the window. She was still there with her gaze transfixed on his window. He looked across at her through the dirty window and smiled again. "Fool, get moving," he said to himself.

At last, his shoes were tied and he reached for his jacket, picked up his keys and pushed hard on the door that led out into the world beyond. The door wouldn't budge. He fumbled with his keys and stuck them into the lock and turned. It was unlocked, but still the door would not open. He stepped back and began to panic. He took a deep breath and looked at the handle. He turned it and pulled. The door opened with ease. Instead of pulling, he had pushed the door before in his haste to get to her.

He rushed down the stairs and grabbed the front door's handle, twisted it and pushed it open.

"Rent, Mr. Shepherd?" Iris, his landlady had come out of her room upon hearing the commotion that he was making. Isaac's hand rested on the handle and slowly pulled it shut.

"Mrs. Henderson" he said with a cheery smile and quickly trying to regain his composure. All the time his thoughts were elsewhere. "I have your money and would be happy to present it to you on my return if that is acceptable to you?"

Iris Henderson bristled at the sound of her name. "It's Miss Henderson as you know only too well, Mr. Shepherd."

"Of course, I apologise." Isaac smiled even though his brain was screaming.

"When you return," she said and closed her door.

Isaac grabbed hold of the door handle and stepped out into the cool air. He took a deep breath, closed his eyes then, as he slowly breathed out, opened his eyes. The young girl was no longer in the park. "No!" he exclaimed.

He scanned the park but could see no sign of her. His heart ached.

"Hello". A small voice startled him. A ringing voice like a sweet song came from behind him. He turned and she stood there with her hands tightly closed around each other for protection.

That wonderful summer's day seemed so long ago now. February 1970 was cold. The winter months marched onwards with frost and regular snow. By the middle of the month, great waves hit the east coast with a fervent fury and Arctic blasts froze the country.

The next month caught the weather forecasters totally unawares. They didn't expect what would come next. Snow!

Early March saw the worst snow for seven years for the same month. On the 4th of March, around twelve inches of snow fell within seven hours the length and breadth of the country. The next day, almost twenty inches of snow landed in the Midlands, with the south seeing almost sixteen inches. Traffic was disrupted up and down the country as schools were closed, factories had to work with just skeleton staff and Britain was almost brought to its knees. A depression moved from the east across much of southern England. Icy rain followed.

The North Sea traffic was still at work though with a much reduced flow of boats traversing the dramatic weather front. Tiny specks disappeared into the gigantic waves, then were thrust skyward with the force of the winds. Isaac watched, as the scene through the window of the watch room took on the quality of a backdrop in a theatre. Painted clouds and a sea awash with fresh paint captured stray ships. Although, this was no painting and the events outside were real. The ferocity of the storm brought a white nightmare of sleet and snow, blinding Isaac with its sheer light. Boats bobbed up and down, straining to keep from capsizing in the maelstrom.

The radio was buzzing with chatter as the Coast Guard contacted the boats and ships, strongly advising them to heave to and head back to port. Most adhered to the commands and struggled with the rough sea and made it to the safety of land. One plucky vessel stayed out: a Norwegian fishing boat who had managed to sneak into England's waters. As the waves lashed the little boat, Isaac couldn't help but think of it as wooden tomb for its crew. The fog horn was working overtime, trying to raise its voice but failing in finding aural supremacy with its battle with the wind. The wind and snow was winning and the outcome of the battle became inevitable. The tiny boat dipped low at the base of a huge wave only to be spat out by the angry ocean as though it was trying dislodge a nasty obstruction. As the boat came down, another wave smashed into its port side, spinning it and crashing it into the sea. Isaac called through to the lifeboat and then the Coast Guard:

"This is Thornside Lighthouse calling Alpha, Charlie, Golf, eight, seven, seven. Calling Alpha, Charlie, Golf, eight, seven, seven. Over"

"This is Alpha, Charlie, Golf, eight, seven, seven. We've seen it Isaac. En route. Over."

"It looks bad, George. I've lost sight of it," Isaac said, struggling with his binoculars. "It took a nasty looking wave straight into its port side and just disappeared. Over."

"We've tried to contact her, but nothing. We contacted them earlier, but I don't think they understood. Over."

"Do what you do, George. Over and out".

Isaac retuned the radio to speak to the Coast Guard. As the radio crackled while he turned the dial he could hear a rhythm beating out over the airwaves which he had never heard before. The distorted sound seemed to be hiding a secret yet was desperate to impart its clandestine voice. Isaac turned the volume up and could hear a steady beat along with very faint music. What was he hearing? He decided against calling the Coast Guard as he had spoken with George and knew that the lifeboat was the only help coming. He clicked off the radio.

Isaac ran up to the watch room and looked out of the window to see if could see anything. Pressing his binoculars to his eyes he watched the scene unfold. The blizzard of snow made it difficult for him to see anything. The Lizzie bounced through the waves towards the stricken fishing boat. Isaac could make out its hull, overturned and helpless. It reminded him of a turtle which had been placed on its back, flaying its legs in the air in a fruitless attempt to right itself. He could just make out the lifeboat crew manning their posts in their normal and organised display. It looked chaotic as the ships tossed and turned to the tune of the sea. As the rescue ship came alongside the turtle, lifebelts were thrown overboard to the Norwegian crew. He could see two of them clinging to the side of the boat as wave after wave battered the boats and crews. The crew of the lifeboat worked together like a well oil machine. The howling wind and drenching sleet didn't deter them from their goal; to save the crew of the fishing boat. After almost fifty minutes struggling with the violent ocean, the lifeboat had all of the men aboard and had fastened tethers to the fishing boat. As they struggled to keep both boats afloat, the weather then did something very unusual. The wind stopped its onslaught. The snow fell slowly and the waves subsided. The sudden change took the crew of the Lizzie by surprise as it shot forward, no longer hindered by the storm. It now moved gracefully towing the little boat behind like a youngster holding its mother's hand. The Lizzie made good use of this unexpected luck, and headed into land as quick as it could. Port was just a few short miles down the coastline and the boat settled itself into a steady yet determined route back to safety. Isaac could see that the deck was a hive of activity with the crew all taking up their stations. The Sun picked out a path in the water as it broke through the dark clouds above. The golden trail lead through to land and George steered his vessel assuredly onward.

"This is Thornside Lighthouse calling Alpha, Charlie, Golf, eight, seven, seven. Calling Alpha, Charlie, Golf, eight, seven, seven. What happened? Over." "This is Alpha, Charlie, Golf, eight, seven, seven. The eye of the storm. Lady luck smiling down on us for a change, Isaac. I'll take it when I can. Going to get this little fellow back to port soon as possible before the weather decides to hit us again. Over." "Good luck, George. Let me know how things go. Over and out."

Isaac headed up stairs to the watch room, grabbed his overcoat, his hat and boots, and stepped out onto the gallery. It was cold, but still. We're in the eye of the storm indeed, thought Isaac. He might have said it out loud, though he couldn't be sure. He was doing that more and more lately and it unnerved him. He looked to where George had steered his brace of ships. He could see them making their way to safety. He then looked up at the sky and saw a swirl of black and grey clouds and the horizon was obscured by a grey blur of snow. Seabirds made use of the surprising lull, and began to dive into the sea to find confused fish swimming close to the surface brought up by the brutal tides just moments before. Isaac thought that the seabirds sounded like babies finding their wailing cry, calling to each other in new voices and diving into the waves to find their easy prey. The fish tossed into the blue sky had no defence from the sharp biting beaks. The little black eyes of the gulls spotted fish after fish in a veritable shooting gallery of food. Their piercing cries grew louder as they swept up and flew passed the lighthouse and back towards their hungry youngsters.

"This isn't going to last," said Isaac, stepping back into the warmth of the lighthouse. Just moments later he could hear the wind singing through the cabling attached to the lightning rod, whistling, whooping and warning. The wind let secrets pass between the rusting cable and the skin of the tower, warning it of the horrors to come. A breath passed between steel and stone.

Then the wind flared up. Sleet and hail battered the lighthouse. Isaac checked the seals of the windows and doors knowing they would do their job, but checking anyway. He would never have needed to do that in the past so why now? He felt as though he had changed recently. Since the terror he felt upon seeing his own silhouette in the glass of the lantern six weeks ago, he had felt different. The dream he'd had, still vivid in his mind had not returned. He dared not look directly at his reflection in the glass lantern since then, especially when the Sun would be behind him. He needed to exorcise this inner demon, and vowed to do it the next time he cleaned the glass. When the weather allowed, he would clean the lantern inside and out. He had kept up with his duties, and always ensured that he didn't have filthy windows. The lamp light would not do its job if the eyes it saw through were not one hundred percent clean. He had washed and dried the windows everyday of his life at the lighthouse, but now made sure that he cleaned six of the windows where the Sun would be in his face and leave the last two a couple of hours before finishing them. He didn't like feeling this way but was at a loss to know what to do. "Keep on keeping on" he thought to himself. The lighthouse had to function no matter how he was feeling. He had a duty and wouldn't let this feeling stop him. He had always been a strong-willed man but this was starting to affect him. Dreams would not halt his desire to continue to live here or to make sure that sailors were safe. The light shone out and gave those passing the feeling of safety and reassurance. That was his goal. That was his reason for being. He glanced over at his bed then to the three photographs which stood side by side on chest of drawers and stroked his grey white beard. The one on the left was of his mother and father on their wedding day. His father, resplendent in his military uniform had his right hand placed firmly on the shoulder of Isaac's beloved mother. The photo was almost sepia in colour now after all these years, but Isaac could clearly see the proud look on his father's face. The frame was a little tarnished now as the silver had begun to peel away. He wished that he had known him.

The middle photograph was taken over thirty years ago on his and Alice's wedding day. They had created a similar pose, but the expressions on both of their faces showed great strain. Was it the strain of Isaac's pending journey into war, perhaps? Or was it the desperation of two people clinging together, trying to find a purpose in their lives?

The last photograph on the right was of him knelt on the grass with his dog, Steam.

That sweet dog of his meant more to him than he realised and a tear fell from his left eye. He had to leave Steam behind with Alice after his marriage had broken down as he couldn't cater for the dog's needs in a lighthouse. It wouldn't have been fair to bring his dog onto this isolated rock. The poor thing died a couple of years ago. He was sixteen years old, one hundred and twelve in dog years. He scanned the three photos and suddenly felt very lonely.

George radioed in to Isaac an hour later to let him know that all hands were safe and sound. They had been fed and watered and the Norwegian crew were now being questioned by the authorities.

The Norwegian fishing boat, the Oseberg had strayed into British fishing waters and had started to caste their nets in the hope of making off with a couple of tonnes of fish. The Coast Guard had been informed by the Sea King helicopter patrolling the skies. Just as the weather had started to worsen, the RNLI lifeboat had been launched and had made its way out to ensure that the Oseberg wouldn't be returning home with British fish. Illegal fishing had been a problem for some years and British fisherman wanted answers. Their livelihood was being threatened by these criminals and something needed to be done. The Coast Guard was well aware of the problems and they were doing their utmost to ensure that these rogue vessels would be deterred from the British waters. The Oseberg was one of many of these boats traversing the North Sea and it wouldn't be the last.

Saving lives hadn't been in the plan of George and his crew, but things can change in an instant on the rough seas and they did what came naturally to them. All hands had been accounted for and would be answering questions for quite a while.

The March weather continued its foray into Britain. For a time on the 7th of March, the Sun dimmed as the moon took a bite out of our life-giving star. The solar eclipse was total over Mexico and the Southern Eastern coast of the United States. In Britain, it just snowed.

Life in the lighthouse was starting to get more difficult for Isaac, but with summer just around the corner, he looked forward to an easier time of things. He always enjoyed living this life but recently, his mind had started to misfire. His dreams had started again. They always followed the same pattern as the first and he couldn't break the cycle.

That night, his sleep was far from restful.

A thunderous crack smashed the door to the lighthouse wide open. The slanting sleet blew mercilessly through the wide open maw. The door seemed to have been ripped from its frame as the wind invited the snow into its new domain. Drifting snow wrapped itself around the base of the lighthouse, penetrating its ice into the rocky foundations. Fragments of the door were imbedded into the surrounding walls and the glass shards from the wrecked windows scattered the snow strewn floor. Isaac stepped through the mess. His feet were bare. Glass and wood cracked beneath his weight and bloody footsteps followed him as he stepped towards the stairs. He looked down at his clothes and saw only his nightshirt, flapping and tattered in the wind. Bone-shaking violent gusts, incessant in their desire to destroy his soul ripped through his body, chilling his frozen core. He turned to look at the door when he reached the bottom of the stairs and saw giant razor like teeth surrounding the gaping ragged hole where the door once offered protection. A shriek rang out into the stormy night and competed with the thunder to reign as the most unholy cataclysmic terror. The crash and screech that accompanied it put an end to the thunders supremacy. A huge explosion came from overhead. Isaac swung around from staring in dismay at the cavity behind him as debris rained down on him. Wind far greater than the mere gusts which had shattered the door to the lighthouse, threw Isaac across the room and into the wall. He pushed himself up off the floor, and headed back towards the stairs. He knew that he to go up those stairs. Whatever was up there, he had to face it. The cold behind him and the heat in front of him made him feel like he was on an unmoving spit, roasting his face, yet freezing his behind. He took one step forwards and upwards. As he reached the first floor smoke filled the room, just like before. He looked around the room to see if he could grab anything to use as a weapon. He reached out for a fire axe leaning against the wall, but as he grabbed it, it crumbled into ash at his touch. There were several coats on the floor near the base of the next set of stairs. He bent down to pick one up, and this too disintegrated into nothing. "This isn't real," he said aloud. "Nothing can hurt me here." With renewed determination, he set forth up to the next floor. He stepped into the room and could see nothing. Fog and smoke swirled around him. As he looked down he couldn't even see his feet. Suddenly, a siren-like scream shot through his ears and he clapped his hands to his ears. Still the sound continued unabated and shook the teeth in his head. A dark silhouette appeared before him. His reflection, come to life. It stood still. The screaming stopped. It took a step forwards. The smoke slowly vanished and Isaac was looking at a grotesque version of himself. The apparition was older than he was now and had a long flowing beard, but his eyes were his. It stepped towards him again. Closer, Isaac could see more clearly that the thing he was looking at was dead. A puppet worked by an invisible master. The marionette then fell straight down into a crumpled heap on the floor and broke into six pieces. Its arms, legs and head detached themselves from the torso and began to spasm in a grisly dance on the floor. Seawater spewed forth from the stumps of the torso, as fish, crabs and assorted sea life crawled out. Isaac could still feel the heat on his face and cowered as the top of the tower ripped off with an almighty eruption. Gruesome gore stained ropes hung down through the smoke. He heard vicious laughter and as the smoke cleared, a huge hand dipped down with ropes tied around each finger and thumb. A skull bracelet dug deep into the wrist of the hand. The heavy anchor chain wrapped tightly around the wrist and Isaac could see that the anchor was still attached and used as a giant clasp to hold the chain in place. The severed heads chattered and gnashed their broken stained teeth at him. The skulls grinned their toothy grin at Isaac as he stared motionless, straining his neck to see further along the arm. The forearms were covered in black tattoos which undulated along the length of the muscle. Huge biceps with scars and scales flexed and twisted. The huge face sneered down at him with its hair on fire and its beard was full of fragmented body parts and blood. Gore dripped down from the straggled beard into the blood red sea below. Its eyes burned into Isaac's soul with all the fire from Hell. Isaac tried to move away just as the malevolent ropes shot down and tightly wrapped around his arms, legs and neck. Sticky with blood they cut into his skin. The devil above screamed with delight and yanked at the ropes. Isaac could see that his head was linked to the fiend's middle finger and his legs were attached to the thumb and little finger. His arms were joined to the other two fingers. As it wiggled his fingers, Isaac pranced and fell to its whim. The giant evil being lifted Isaac up to its ghastly face. Bloody snakes slithered through its teeth and flicked their black tongues out at Isaac.

"Isaac!" its shrill voice hurt his ears. "Isaac Shepherd." The "s" of his Christian name was hissed and mocked. Drool and blood dripped out of the corners of its mouth as it spoke. Sharp broken teeth filled its mouth.

"Killer!" it shouted. Its voice sounded as though it had split in two between a high pitched voice and a deep grave growl. Tears streamed down Isaac's face from the heat and the ghastly spectre.

"What?" Isaac mewed.

"Inhuman sadistic murderer," it shrieked its demonic laugh.

With a sharp tug of the ropes, Isaac was pulled into the air passed the squealing skulls and up to meet his captors eyes.

Isaac's body jerked out of bed. He sat up and cradled his head in his hands. Tears rolled down his face as he tried to think why his brain was doing this to him. Why was he dreaming such horrors? He had never had these dreams never mind those evil thoughts in his head that must have created them. He shakily got out of bed and stepped into the bathroom. Isaac looked in the mirror. His blood froze at what he saw. His hair was totally white. Yesterday, it was grey with flecks of white, but not today. But that wasn't the only reason that he had gasped. Isaac had two lines cut deep into his forehead angling down from his hairline to touch his eyebrows. He carefully touched the one on the right where he felt a sharp pain. He ran his finger down to his bushy eyebrow and could feel the trench there. They were new wrinkles which made him look a hundred years older. He moved his face closer to the mirror for a better look. More lines covered his face. He tried to smile and saw four thick grooves emanating from the corner of his eyes fanning out towards his ears. As he lowered his mouth more lines appeared. He thought it made him look like a ventriloquists dummy as thick, black lines creased from each corner of this mouth to make it look like his chin was a separate appendage. He opened his mouth a couple of times, clacking his teeth each time. His jaw come loose and fell to the floor exposing sharp pointed teeth.

The dream's climax threw him back into reality. He lay there looking at the ceiling. He dare not move. Gradually, Isaac lifted his arms. He sat up. Looking around his room and he saw nothing out of place, nothing wrong. Slowly, gently, he pulled back the covers and looked down at his body. Fine, nothing wrong there. He gingerly placed his feet on the floor and stood up. Swaying slightly, he took hold of the chair by his bed. He let go and stretched his arms above him and stood on his tiptoes. "Am I awake?" he said aloud. He felt awake. He hurt all over, so he assumed he was. His face was wet with tears he didn't remember crying. He needed to wash his face and get his head clear. Steeping into the bathroom, his feet touched the cold linoleum bringing him round a bit more. He didn't turn on the light for fear of seeing what the dream might have done to his face. He turned on the cold tap, tilted his head so the water trickled down his face and let the water wash across his mouth. He took the glass from the cabinet and filled it with cool water. He drank it down in one. He went to sit on the edge of his bed and wiped away his tears when his head started to ache. The clock said two forty five; the same time as before. Was there any significance behind the time? He needed to sleep, so he lay back down on the bed and brought the cover up and over his head. His eyes stung and his head ached. The dim glow from his bed-side light cast a mesh shadow over his face. Isaac turned off the light by the bed and settled down to sleep.

A shadow caught Isaac's eye. It moved slowly around the room before settling on his father's chest of drawers. He tried to focus his eyes on the black mass but could not make out what it was or where the shadow had come from. His skin began to prickle as a breeze touched him ever so gently.

He reached for the light switch then stopped. He shifted his vision around the room and the shadow followed his gaze. He blinked and the image became a white negative in his mind. He blinked quicker to try and catch a clear picture of the shadow but each time it flashed all too briefly before disappearing. He turned on the light again and looked around his room. Nothing new met his weary eyes and when he blinked the image faintly faded from his dark view.

His mind was still wired after the events of his nightmare. He knew that there was nothing in his room with him but he still felt uneasy and tired. Not since he was a child had he contemplated leaving on the light. But tonight he felt he needed the comfort of the night light. He closed his eyes tightly then immediately regretted it knowing that he would have to peel back his eye-lids and face the room again. It had been his sanctuary for so long but was now starting to feel like a prison. His brain took over and brought some sense and a little bravery back to his mind and body. He opened his eyes and began to settle back down into his warm bed and he turned off his light. The sudden darkness enveloped him before the curtain allowed shards of white moon light to dance over the walls and furniture of his room. "Shadows everywhere," thought Isaac.

"Damn fool" he said aloud and closed his eyes.

CHAPTER THREE

Another visitor

Another life

Who sees what's real?

Who sees the lies?

The birds woke him up and he looked at his clock. It was five o'clock the following morning. He got out of bed and went to the bathroom to get ready for the day ahead and tried to forget his nightmare of the night before. He would be getting some fresh supplies today when Peter would visit. Peter would be bringing the fuel, food and other provisions Isaac needed to run the lighthouse. Peter Ambrose was a pleasant man in his mid forties and Isaac looked forward to his cheery conversations with him. He needed it after the night he had just had.

He plucked up the courage to look in the mirror. His eyes focused on his grey and white head of hair. It was not the pure white like his dream would have had him believe. He reached up and touched the deep line on his forehead which met his eyebrows but felt no pain. These were new wrinkles. He hadn't noticed them previously, but then again he didn't usually have any reason to study his face. He knew what he looked like well enough. Again, he moved his face closer to the mirror for a better look. He tried to smile and saw no sign of any new wrinkles there. He touched his mouth and looked for any new lines. No new line there. He slowly opened his mouth. His teeth! A black hole greeted him when he opened his mouth fully. His front four teeth at the bottom were black. He vigorously brushed away the filth attacking his mouth. Black red splashes splattered the white sink. Once he had brushed away all that he could see he swilled his mouth out with cold water. Pink water fell from his mouth into the sink. Blood! Another mouthful and the water was clear. He got closer to the mirror to take a look at what had caused the blood. There were no cuts or any sign of bleeding.

As he ate his breakfast, his mind worked on what he was going to do. He had gone through two terrifying dreams in the last couple of months and it was taking its toll on him. He never had problems sleeping, so what had changed? This year started really cold with winter weather stretching all the way through to April. Heavy snow back in March had made life for everyone in Britain and they had coped. Why wasn't Isaac coping as well as the rest of the country? Was it the stress of working alone in a lighthouse? He'd done it for twelve years and seen really bad weather back in 1963 and some of the years that following had horrendous winters. He had been drinking a bit more of late, but he could handle that. Anyway, Peter would be bringing him a few more whiskey bottles today. "And some food," Isaac reminding himself. Should he speak to Peter about what had been happening lately or bottle it up? He decided to keep this to himself.

He needed to relax. Paint, he thought. It always gave him time away from his thoughts. His paintings sold well back at shore and Peter would collect his latest ones and get them framed in Bridlington. He would then take them from town to town up and down the east coast and would display them on his boat when he moored in the harbour. He and Isaac would split the proceeds with Isaac getting the lion's share of eighty percent of the profits. After all, he did the painting. Peter was a good salesman but only as good as the wares he had to trade. The quality of Isaac's painting was never in doubt and Peter rarely came back with any unsold.

Two boats bobbed up and down in the blue and white crested waves. Isaac sketched the boats onto his pad. The pencil lined drawing would be used as a template for the details he would later add to his painting. Now, he had to get the movements right in his picture. Waves took hold of the ship's bow as it crashed onwards through the waves. He lovingly swept the knife over the canvas creating dark foreboding clouds. Outside, the Sun's rays streaked down to the dramatic sea below. He added more paint to canvas and stood back. From the safety of his room he could see that the captain of the larger ship had talent. He cut and chopped through the waves with such panache. It was a pleasure for Isaac to witness. Even though the window was small, he had a good view.

"Ahoy there". Peter's arrival was a very welcoming sight. Isaac put down his palette knife and covered the painting with a cloth cover and went to help Peter bring in the monthly supplies.

"Food, fresh blankets, towels, beer, fuel and whiskey," beamed Peter, and then the smile dropped.

"My god, what happened to you, Isaac?" Peter's face quickly changed from one of carefree happiness into one of abject horror and concern.

Isaac's face mirrored his friend's concern as he touched the fresh creases on his forehead.

I'm fine, Pete, I just had a rough sleep last night." Isaac tried to explain away his new wrinkles.

"Sorry, Isaac, but you look terrible. I'm telling you this as a friend so don't take any offence."

"It's fine, Pete, don't worry."

Isaac tried to force a smile and took the boxes and packages from Peter and placed them on the kitchen floor. Peter followed with the fuel.

"What do you say that we get this stuff put away and have a cup of tea?" Isaac offered.

"Good idea, let's go." Peter glanced at Isaac and shrugged. Something's wrong, though Peter.

Within twenty minutes, the two of them stood in the doorway looking out to sea. Both held a steaming mug of black tea in their labourers' hands watching the seagulls feed and fly down from the cliffs. Skilfully gliding close to the water, they skimmed and swooped down in the icy cold sea. Four of them hit the water, one after another like darts hitting a dart board. They dived deep and came up with small morsels of food for their young waiting with mouths wide open in their nests high up on the cliffs. Crying and screeching, they called to each other. They seemed to be flying wildly, trying to search for their own nest before landing gently at the right outcrop.

"I never tire watching those birds. How free they look. This is the life," said Isaac with a distant look on his face.

"What is wrong?" a concerned Peter asked.

"Nothing, everything's alright," Isaac lied. Should he tell his friend that he had a vision and a dream? No, it sounded crazy, but then again, maybe he was crazy.

"Look," began Peter. "I've known you for a very long time and I can see that something is either worrying you or something has happened." Isaac could tell that Peter wasn't going to let this go.

"I'm fine, I told you!" Isaac snapped back at Peter.

Peter saw a look on his friend's face that he had never seen before. Isaac was good-natured and easy-going. This wasn't like him to act in such an aggressive way.

"I'm sorry, Pete, I shouldn't have…" began Isaac.

"It's alright, but you need to unload things. I want to help if I can." Peter interrupted.

Isaac stared out to sea. He brought the mug of tea to his dry lips and took a sip. His hands trembled. Peter watched him. He could see by Isaac's body language that his friend was in torment. Leave it, he'll tell me when he's ready, thought Peter.

"I saw something," Isaac finally said.

Peter said nothing as Isaac turned to face him.

"Something in the lantern's glass," he said as his eyes searched out his feet. The empty mug loosely hung at his side and his body went limp.

Peter caught him as he fell forwards.

"Steady, come on." Peter helped Isaac back indoors and set him down in the large chair.

Isaac's head felt heavy and dizzy as he sat there in a daze. His hazy vision was starting to improve as he looked up at Peter.

Without any mote hesitation, Isaac looked up and finally said the word that burned his lips: "Ghosts!"

Peter froze and studied Isaac's face. It was pale and he looked much older than his fifty three years. All of life's worries were etched in deep lines across his features. Peter knelt down and faced Isaac.

"Ghost?" repeated Peter.

"Something very odd is happening to me, Pete. I saw something in the glass of the lantern, a dark entity; a shadow, a reflection of me that wasn't me." Isaac looked straight into Peter's frightened eyes. "It was evil."

Peter looked away and around the room. Everything looked normal. He looked at the small kitchen with its stove and small fridge, pots, pans and discarded plates; a picture of domesticity. Then, in the middle of it all was Isaac. He could see that he was in turmoil and in need of a friend.

"Isaac," Peter spoke calmly. "There are no such things as ghosts. Tell me what you saw."

Isaac told him of the strange reflection and of the cold fear he felt. Speaking about it gave him the courage to continue.

"Then, there was the dream," Isaac went on. He told Peter of the creature that had attacked him and of the bodies and the fire.

"Your imagination is running riot," said Peter after hearing of Isaac's terrifying nightmare. "You need some company. What do you say about having a house guest tonight? I can stay over if you need me to."

Isaac looked at him and he felt a wave of emotion come over him. He smiled a broad and grateful smile.

"Wonderful," He sighed.

Isaac felt like crying again. What was wrong with him? He was a grown man. Everyone needs to spend time with another human being, even just to make you realise you're not alone in this world.

"Look, it's six thirty and I have to get back to shore, load up the van, and take some more supplies up to the lighthouse at Flamborough. They're not stuck on a rock in the North Sea like you are, but they still need supplies. They get some stuff locally, but I can get them the good stuff at cheaper prices. I have a few errands to do in Whitby, so that'll take me a good four or five hours. I'll get back here for about two this afternoon, and I can help you get the lighthouse ready for tonight. What do you say?"

"Sounds really good. I'll get a couple of fish ready for us. A few of those potatoes you've brought will make fine chips". Isaac was relieved and looked forward to some company. He felt like he had another purpose other than manning the lighthouse. His friend was coming to stay.

"Right. I'll fetch some more fine bottles of beer for us for when we've finished the chores tonight," Peter winked.

"Be safe," shouted Isaac as Peter's little boat pulled away. Peter give him a sharp salute, then pointed towards to open sea. "Onwards and don't worry about a thing," he shouted.

Isaac smiled.

Isaac felt much better after Peter's visit. Just talking to another person had really helped. He felt stupid saying to someone that he'd had a bad dream.

How old was he?

But the dreams had shaken him.

Brush it off, and get yourself sorted out, he thought.

He busied himself sorting through the supplies that Peter had brought. The fuel had been stored and the empties loaded back on Peter's boat. The food packages had been placed in the pantry next to the kitchen and clean sheets, linen and towels were put away. The Coast Guard had passed by earlier and George had radioed in to see how things were going. Isaac needed that. First seeing Peter, then a call from George. He was starting to feel more human again and last night's nightmare had passed from his mind. He stood again in the doorway, watching the birds. The rocks glistened with the spray from the sea and a rainbow shimmered in the above the water. The air felt cool but not as icy as the early morning. He walked around the base of the lighthouse to the boathouse stationed to the right of the tower. His own boat bobbed about inside, tethered safely to the hook inside. He held onto the hand rail and looked out to sea.

The sea had settled down now and he watched two ships sail calmly by. He took three deep breaths and filled his lungs with the salty sea air. This is what he lived for.

Painting had always been his passion. Drawing, sketching, pastels, crayons, charcoal, paints or ink, he had tried them all. He had enjoyed it since he was a boy. Getting hold of the material had proved difficult over the years, but he had made do with whatever he could find. Paper had been in short supply, so he had sketched on wooden boxes. When he was only four-years old he would draw on the walls of his mother's house. He had three of his paintings in his bedroom. As his life had been the lighthouse it was no surprise that his main theme was the sea. He enjoyed painting it in all seasons. The heavy leaden sky and grey black seas throughout autumn. The white snow along with storms came in winter. Spring brought white grey clouds with some light rain which looked like tiny jewels breaking the surface of the sea. Summer showed blue skies and an even bluer sea. He loved the white crashing waves hitting the rocks of his home or the rocks and cliffs behind the lighthouse. He had plenty of time on this rock in the sea to indulge in his favourite hobby.

Isaac sat in front of his easel. He had tried his hand at oil painting and water colours though preferred to use a palette knife. He had mounted the board and applied a light brown wash with his brush. The wash covered the board ready for painting. He looked at his earlier effort of the two boats and sky, then turned his attention back to the paints. The palette had been loaded with oils of his favourite persuasion. Burnt umber, mixing white, zinc white, lemon yellow, cobalt blue, light green, light cadmium red and ivory black. The eight spots of paint sat waiting patiently to be used and mixed. He reached for the knife and started to mix the colours to his desired taste. He deftly and confidently put knife to canvas and began to load on the colours. He looked out of the door to the view outside. The waves were gentle and the sky blue with few clouds. The cliffs to the north which sheltered the bay from the strongest of winds cut deep into the sea. Its prominent cliffs stood majestically surveying the ocean beyond. Isaac scanned from north to south and took in the serene scene before him. Again, the palette knife skimmed across the sheet in front of him. The blue grey sea contrasted with the bright blue and white sky above. A flock of birds crossed his view and he quickly gave two knife strokes to the canvas for each flying creature. Two upward strokes at an obtuse angle for most, a more acute angle for others. He enjoyed putting life onto the canvas as it happened. The dark clouds which had painted before had moved on, but he kept them in their anyway.

He turned on the radio to catch the forecast.

"And now the Shipping Forecast..." Isaac listened to the rest of the forecast hoping for a change of fortune.

"There are warnings of gales in Viking, Forties, Cromarty, Forth, Fisher, Dover, Wight, Portland, Plymouth, Finisterre, Sole, Lundy, Fastnet, Rockall, Malin, Hebrides, Bailey, Fair Isle, Faroes and Southeast Iceland.

The general synopsis at one eight double-O: low just north of Viking, nine double-seven, moving steadily east-northeast.

Low three hundred miles south of Iceland. Atlantic flow forming, moving steadily northeast.

A ridge of high pressure has swayed between North and South Utsire. The area forecast for the next twenty-four hours. Viking, Forties, Cromarty, Forth."

He switched off the radio. It was going to get rough later with a storm coming in from the northeast and Isaac was going to be busy. Painting would have to wait. Never anything to do, then you make yourself busy, he thought and chuckled. He was beginning to feel much better.

He had to catch lunch so he went to retrieve his fishing rod. Isaac cast his line and saw the hook cut through the surface and the float bobbed gently in the rocking waves. He sat there pondering his life. He enjoyed life out here on the rocks in his tower. He considered the lighthouse to be his as it had been his home for so long now. The time he had spent living in the little house with his ex-wife wasn't the best time of his life. It had been cramped and Alice wasn't really the happy housewife he hoped she would be. He remembered Steam, his dog, bounding through from room to room investigating and sniffing as he went. He loved that dog. He hardly ever barked and his tail never stopped wagging. Isaac called it his "Wigger Wagger" and Steam seemed loved that.

The float danced around the waves until suddenly it disappeared beneath the froth. Isaac stood up and began to gently play with the line slowly, carefully, reeling in his catch. The thrashing skate flapped about as he hauled it over the rocks and into the bucket which sat on the path. He gently unhooked the fish and examined it. It was only a young fish. He walked down to the rocks and placed it back into the sea. "Come back in a month and you'll be fine for frying," he called after it.

He cast the line back into the sea and stood watching the little float sit there waiting to fulfil its role and inform Isaac that lunch will be served. It didn't have long to wait for some more action. It dipped down again and Isaac whipped it back out as soon as it moved. The salmon pulled and fought to escape but to no avail. Isaac brought it straight to the bucket and took the hook out of its mouth.

"One more to go," he said.

After another three minutes the salmon had company in the bucket and he and Peter would eat well this afternoon.

As Isaac prepared the fish, he felt as though a weight had been lifted from his shoulders. He even started to whistle. He had the radio playing Radio One for a change. "The Radio 1 Club with Dave Cash" had just finished and Tony Brandon came on. The first song he played was Ireland's first ever Eurovision Song Contest winner. "All Kinds of Everything" by Dana flowed out of the speakers, and warmed Isaac's heart. He felt that he needed a change of pace. Dana gave way to B.J.William saying that "Raindrops Keep Fallin' on My Head".

"Makes a change from the snow," Isaac smiled to himself. His mind wandered and thought of his father. "William Shepherd, what were you like?" he said aloud.

It was a quarter past two when he heard the familiar sound of Peter's little boat chug through the water. The chips splashed and fought for freedom in Isaac's pan and the fish smelt wonderful. He had lightly grilled the fish so to try and keep in some flavour.

"Ahoy there, shipmate," called Peter.

"Hey Peter," Isaac shouted back.

As promised, Peter had brought some beer bottles back with along with a large bottle of Scotch Whiskey. He carried a duffel bag containing a roll up bed and fresh clothes. "£3.25 that cost me," joked Peter. "We'll sink that tonight".

Isaac laughed. It was good to hear that noise, he thought. It's been a while.

"How are you doing now, old friend?" asked Peter, as he heard the unusual sounds of contemporary music filling the lighthouse.

"Better. Thank you Pete."

"I thought it seemed strange that you were listening to Radio One. Was it a mistake?"

"I felt like a change. I wanted to hear what all the fuss was about," replied Isaac.

"There are a lot of good bands out there, you know. It's not all about the classics anymore. I heard of a new group that sings about elves and dragon. All acoustic guitar and bongos."

"Sounds odd," laughed Isaac.

"They've called Tyrannosaurus Rex. Very cool".

"Yes, very cool," mocked Isaac. "Wasn't that a dinosaur?"

"No, you're the only dinosaur around here." Peter laughed.

"And I call you a friend! I've been doing a little thinking, Pete."

"Careful there, you don't want to blow a gasket. Food smells good."

Not just yet, thought Isaac.

Peter sat himself at the small table and picked up the fork and knife.

"Nearly ready?"

This was a good idea, thought Isaac. He felt as though he had been slipping into a dark place, and that wasn't good.

He began to plate up the meal, and placed a big mug of steaming tea in front of Peter.

"Enjoy," he said as he set their plates down.

"Sorry, no milk, Pete. I don't drink it."

"I know that. I'm the one who brings you what you do need, remember?" smiled Peter.

The door was open, and the seagulls were continuing to feed their young. Having his friend here and good food in his belly made him start to forget about the troubles his mind had been conjuring up. He cleared the table and filled the sink. Hot water burned through the grease on the plates as they slid beneath the frothy surface. "All in the mind," he thought to himself.

"Let's get cracking then" said Peter. "Where do you want to start?"

"Why don't you put your boat into the boat-house and tether it tight. The weather's not bad now, but it's due to turn tonight," replied Isaac.

Peter leapt onto his boat and steered it around to the right hand side of the tower, unlocked the door to the boat house and pushed it in. He made it secure, and walked on the rock path back around to the main door.

Isaac had washed up and put everything away as Peter joined him in the kitchen area. "Bridge over troubled water" was playing on the radio when Isaac turned it off.

"Right, we need to make sure that we contact the Coast Guard to check what ships are coming through the bay and we need to prepare the lantern for tonight. There is no fog forecast for tonight, but we need to ensure that the horns are clear and we need to do a test".

"Right," saluted Peter. "Let's jump to it."

Isaac went over to the radio and checked in with the Coast Guard. Four vessels would be coming through this afternoon with two more in the evening. The Lizzie was on stand-by should there be any problems. George and his crew were always ready for anything. He reported that there would be five ships and boats passing through between midnight and six the following morning. Isaac wrote down the information in his book.

Isaac prepared a bucket of soapy water and three cloths to clean the glass and the lantern. They moved upward, through the lighthouse tower. As they made their way into the lantern room, Peter stopped and asked, "What was the dream?"

Isaac paused, his back to Peter.

"I can't really remember it".

"It had you shaken up badly. You do remember."

"Yes, but I feel better now. I don't need to go over it again."

"It might help," Peter said.

Isaac turned and put the bucket down.

"Fire, the Devil, pain, the usual things that nightmares are made of."

"Tell me."

Isaac looked out of the window and began to tell Peter what he'd dreamt.

Peter listened and watched him as he enlightened Peter with the details. When he had finished, he faced Peter to see the look of apprehension on his face.

"There you have it."

"Right. Okay. So…you've had this twice?"

"Yes, but different both times. Last night's was the worst."

"Any idea what it might mean?"

"That I'm going crazy."

"You're not; it's just a weird set of thoughts going through your head. Look, I can stay tonight and tomorrow if you need some company. I told my wife that I'd be staying here tonight, but I'm sure she'd be okay for another night. I think you need a friend around to help with the burden of running this place. I can't remember you ever having a holiday or even a break in the years I've known you."

He was right. Isaac only lived for the lighthouse. It had been his home now for twelve years and, up until a few weeks ago, he had enjoyed his time here. Company would be good for a couple of days, but he just wanted to see how he went today. From being own his own all the time to sharing his home with someone, if only for one night, might be a bit much. He didn't want to turn Pete's offer down though.

"Thanks Pete. That'd be really good of you. As long as your wife doesn't mind."

"She'll be fine. Look, let's get these jobs done and then listen to "I'm sorry, I'll read that again". Da da da dummm." Beethoven would turn in his grave if he knew that his wonderful fifth symphony piece of music was now linked to a comedy show.

Isaac smiled. "Good idea."

Isaac started to clean the lenses of the lantern whilst Peter concentrated on the glass outside. Isaac couldn't stomach washing the outer windows for the fear of maybe seeing that reflection again. The thought was still with him, even though he was feeling much better about things. As he washed and polished, he nodded to Peter who was making his way around the outside of the lantern. He threw the remnants of the water over the last pieces of glass and stood there watching the cascade. As Peter lifted his arm to start washing the glass he stopped and stared. He had a quizzical look on his face which then turned to revulsion. Isaac stopped and looked at him. The Sun was behind Peter and Isaac too froze. What is he seeing? thought Isaac. Peter looked straight through him.

"Peter," Isaac shouted and put his hands on the glass. Peter didn't move. Isaac rushed out to meet his friend outside but could not open the door. He pulled at the handle but the door wouldn't budge. Frantically, he tugged until the door came loose and he rushed out on to the gallery. As he turned to face Peter, he saw a black shape emanating from the window. The evil shadow reached out for Peter as Isaac ran to his friend. As he grabbed hold of Peter's shoulders, his friend went limp and fell to the metal floor. Looking up, he saw the shadow retreat into the glass leaving a dark smudge. He lifted Peter by getting his head under one shoulder and then he dragged him down the steps and into the watch room.

He laid Peter on the floor and went to the bathroom to fetch some water. He propped him up in the chair and brought the water to his lips. Peter looked pale but his tongue came out to feel the cool liquid. He moved his head forward to get a drink and his eyes opened.

"What happened, Isaac?" he asked feebly.

"You fell. Are you alright?"

"A little woozy and my eyes hurt. I'm okay, really."

"You took a nasty turn out there. Do you know what happened?" Isaac wanted to hear Peter's take on what he saw.

"I think I was blinded by the Sun's reflection in the glass. As I looked up, I felt light-headed. Did I fall?"

"Yes, but you're inside now. You're safe." Isaac didn't like the sound of that.

"Thanks. Could I have some more water, Isaac?"

"Yes, I'll get it."

Isaac went to the bathroom and filled the glass. He looked at his own reflection which looked back with a knowing look on its face. He'd seen it and Peter had seen it although he doesn't seem to remember.

"There you go," he passed the glass to Peter who had started to come around.

"Do you have anything for a headache?"

"Relax, I'll get you some tablets. Take another drink."

Peter sat on the chair facing the door at the base of the lighthouse, sipping at a mug of tea. A little whiskey had been poured in, just to calm him down. I saw it, thought Isaac.

"How are you feeling now, Pete," asked Isaac.

"Better, much better, thanks. I haven't a clue what happened there. I'm sorry to have scared you like that."

"Did you see anything at all strange?" Isaac had not told Peter about the ominous reflection he had seen some weeks ago.

"No. Why?"

"I saw you before you fell, and you seemed transfixed with something." Isaac didn't like the fact that his friend had not seen the shadow. But, he must have.

"Nothing at all. Sun blindness, I think that was all. Don't look so worried, I feel fine now and this whiskey is doing the trick."

"Good. Put your feet up and enjoy your tea." Isaac stood up and decided to go and have a look at the window again. He felt stronger now and more determined.

Climbing the steps, Isaac didn't feel as confident as he had in the warmth of the lighthouse. His bravado started to slip but he carried on regardless. With each step he made his legs felt as though an extra weight had been added to them. By the time he reached the top he ached all over. Something was sapping his strength. Still he moved on. As he reached the window where his friend had fallen and the spectre had reached out for him he feared for what he might see. Stepping carefully to the side of the glass he tried to see if there was any mark. Nothing, not a scratch or a smudge, just dry water marks where Peter had thrown the last splashes of the bucket. He took out the cloth and wiped the glass clean. He stood back against the railings and observed the surface. He couldn't see anything wrong at all. Moving from window to window he checked each of the eight pieces of glass for anything untoward. He carefully wiped each surface clean and inspected them closely. He found no evidence of any marks whatsoever. He felt a little better but the underlining feeling of dread hung over him. He then went back inside to complete cleaning the lenses. He checked the bulbs and they were all in place and working fine. That just left the fog horn, he thought. His practical organised self came to the fore as he started back down to see how Peter was doing. He then felt a new threat. Was Peter going to be there?

He moved as quickly as he dared, making sure he didn't fall or stumble in his rush. He rapidly moved down to the ground floor to find Peter gone. He frantically looked outside for him but there was no sign. He then heard the flush of the toilet and Peter stepped out.

"Do you have anything to make the toilet smell better?"

Isaac could have hugged him.

"Just keep the door open. The sea air will do its job. You okay?"

"I am now" Peter laughed. "What are you making tonight, I'm starving."

"Hey, take it easy. You'll be fed and watered, don't you worry". Isaac was the one who was worried. Peter seemed to be alright, but he still looked pale.

"I need to check the fog horn then I'll crack open a beer for you. How does that sound?"

"Great, even though it's a little early for me."

Isaac looked at his watch. It was five fifteen. Not too early for me, he thought.

Isaac stepped out into the darkness with his flashlight. He should have done this earlier, but with Peter's incident he just hadn't found the time. He walked around to the fog horn room attached to the front of the lighthouse. The three horns faced out to sea and Isaac reached up to feel inside each of them to see if there was an obstruction. No, they're fine, he concluded after checking all three. You never knew when a stupid seagull would decide to make a new nest in one of them. He unlocked the door and stepped inside. He checked the sensor and the power. Everything was okay here as well. "It's about time something went right," he said. Locking the door, he looked out to sea and saw a ship making its way north. He waved. "Done it again" he said.

He made his way back around to the door where Peter greeted him.

"Everything ship shape skipper?" he beamed.

"Just about. I just need to give a quick blast of the horn and get the lantern up and running." He closed the door tight.

Peter looked a lot better now as he turned on the radio to hear the familiar

Beethoven's Fifth Symphony singing out as Isaac gave a blast on the fog horn. "I'm sorry, I'll read that again" was in full flow. The deep voices of the horns boomed out over the ocean. After getting the lantern in motion, Isaac allowed himself a beer. He fetched two bottles from the fridge, flipped the caps off and handed one to Peter. "Cheers!" he said as they clinked the bottles together.

For the next twenty minutes they laughed at the cast of the radio show. Isaac made a few sandwiches of ham and pickle and settled down with another beer. Peter seemed to be absolutely fine now and had laughed heartily to Bill Oddie's song about Angus Prune. He always liked that. Then the song "There was a ship set that put to sea all in the month of May" started and Peter sang along but singing the right words instead of the parody now playing on the radio. The old folk song "Soon May The Wellerman Come" had been a firm favourite of his in his youth.

"Not quite Alan Cooper is it?" said Isaac.

"ALICE Cooper" cried Peter. He started to choke on his beer. They both laughed and Peter had tears rolling down his cheeks. Isaac watched him carefully over the top of his beer bottle. Peter was a good man and he'd come over to keep Isaac company. Isaac felt guilty at accepting his offer to stay as he'd taken a nasty fall and a fright which Peter now obviously didn't remember.

"What's on the box tonight?" asked Peter as Isaac flicked through the new Radio Times which Peter had brought with him.

"Well, there's "Softly Softly Task Force" on at eight on BBC One, or "The High Chaparall" on BBC Two. I'm not much of a snooker fan, but "Pot Black" is on later. You can see the different colours of the balls now. Much better than black and white."

"Do you think that they'll ever be anything good on that thing? We still have a black and white one at home."

A sudden clap of thunder snapped them out of the Radio Times. The room lit up with the flash of lightning that followed four seconds afterwards.

"That's two miles away," said Isaac leaping up to grab the radio.

"Thornside Lighthouse calling Alpha, Charlie, Golf, eight, seven, seven. Calling Alpha, Charlie, Golf, eight, seven, seven. Over".

Static…

"Thornside Lighthouse calling Alpha, Charlie, Golf, eight, seven, seven. Calling Alpha, Charlie, Golf, eight, seven, seven. George, can you hear me. Over".

"This is…… seven…….Isaac……ver"

"George, can you hear me?" Isaac said again.

"Isaac, I can just……The weather……us hard……so……a thing……Over"

"You're breaking up, George. Try again. Over" Isaac couldn't hide the panic in his voice.

"Isaac, the weather had hit us really hard. We have hail……waves are getting very high out here……………."

The fog horn came to life and gave three destructive blasts. Isaac could see the lighthouse's lantern spreading its light over the sea at into a black mass of heavy thunder clouds. They seem to hang there, waiting to impart some devastating power. Light flashed and he could make out The Lizzie heave and ride the high waves. The rain and hail was confined to the sea and hadn't hit the lighthouse yet. Isaac felt helpless as he saw the boat rise and fall. Its light flickered and died as a huge wave crashed into it head on. The hull gave way and the pilot's cabin caved in. A bright explosion flashed as a lightning bolt struck the boat. The boat tossed and spun through the cruel sea splintering it apart bit by bit. The boat was ripped into pieces by the onslaught of the sea and hail. Winds whipped round the carcass like carrion crows feeding on the dead. Isaac watched in terror as the boat disappeared.

"George!" he shouted. He knew there would be no answer. "No! No! No! No! No!" he wailed.

As soon as it appeared, the storm shifted off and out into the dark, leaving flashes as a reminder of what carnage it had left behind.

"Isaac," said Peter. "What happened?"

"They've gone. The boat, the crew. George."

"My God. But the storm, it's gone."

CHAPTER FOUR

Is it a phantom?

A trick of the eye

A ghostly shadow

Is it time to die?

Alice and Isaac had married on Thursday the 2nd of September 1939, one day before he went to war. It was a simple yet beautiful wedding. The months prior to the war had been magical for him as this young girl had fallen for him in the same way he had fallen for her. Isaac's mother attended their wedding but his father, William Shepherd had died back in 1918 during his time fighting in the First World War. Isaac had been one year old at the time. Almost four months after his death the war ended on the 11th of November 1918 with Germany ordering a cease-fire.

His father had been in the Navy and had served on one of the first aircraft carriers utilised in war, the HMS Fury. It was this aircraft carrier that launched the Sopwith Camels that were sent to attack the great Zeppelin hangers based at Tondern in Germany. The aim was to turn the war to the allies' advantage. The raid was code-named Operation F6. After an unsuccessful attempt to attack the airships at the end of June was cancelled due to terrible winds, the attacks were rescheduled for the 17th of July 1918. The new venture was renamed Operation F7 and this time it had to be a success. Despite a heavy thunder storm and a delay, the eight planes were launched and attacked the three airship sheds early that morning in two waves. They managed to destroy two large Zeppelins, L54 and L60 with four of the enemy suffering fatal injuries during the raid. On its return journey to Southampton, a squadron of German planes attacked the HMS Fury. In the attack all German planes were shot down, although sadly, five British sailors lost their lives. William was one of the sailors.

Dark days followed the death of George and his crew. The Sea King helicopter had been sent into the storm to try and rescue any survivors. The helicopter had been told to abort its first attempt as the winds and hail beat down hard on its blades. There was no way the helicopters crew would go back to base. There were friends in the cold sea and the crew of the Sea King forged on through the storm. There were none found alive. Only two bodies had been recovered. It was the first loss of a life boat in these waters and it had proved to be a catastrophic loss of lives. George Meade, Charlie Douglas, Andrew Smeaton, Warren Forester, Richard "Dickie" Davidson and Robert Chamberlain had all lost their lives that night. Only Charlie and "Dickie" were pulled out of the water almost an hour after the boat had been struck. The Lizzie had been totally destroyed. There was nothing left.

The loss of the men had a terrible effect on Peter. He knew each of the brave men and had gone to school with George, Andrew, "Dickie" and Robert. They had grown up around Bridlington and they had remained firm friends. Peter had tried to join the RNLI with his associates, but as he had asthma he had failed the medical exam. As his school buddies joined up and found themselves serving on the same vessel, Peter continued to work on land. He had managed to get the job of delivery man and would drive between towns delivering supplies and food to businesses. The only time he would need to use a boat was to deliver to the lighthouse. This is how he came to know Isaac.

To Isaac, George had been a voice on the radio and as distant as Tony

Hancock or The Goons. He had never met him or even spoken to any of the other men in George's crew, but he felt an affinity with them. They were in the same job of helping people and trying to save lives. The six men had lost their lives patrolling an area where no other vessels were threatened. They were doing their job and the weather destroyed them in the process.

That night, Peter and Isaac sat in silence staring into the bleak distance. It was supposed to have been a chance for Isaac to have some friendship and company. With Peter's incident earlier in the day and the death of six men, today had come to a tragic end. Isaac sipped at his whiskey as Peter idly swirled the liquid around in his glass. It was Isaac who broke the silence.

"It shouldn't have happened." Isaac's voice sounded distant.

Peter looked up in a daze.

"Sorry?"

"There was no reason for them to be out there. The ships that were scheduled to pass had diverted east to miss the storm. Why were they patrolling?"

"They were professionals and checking the area," answered Peter.

"But that put them in danger. No, there must have been a good reason for them to be there."

Isaac reached for the radio and called the Coast Guard head quarters.

He spoke to the operator and asked if George had radioed in before the storm took them.

"We had a message from him saying that he was picking up a faint signal and was going to investigate. They had a reading on the radar but couldn't pin point the exact spot," said Tom, the chief operator back at the Coast Guard head quarters.

"Did he receive a distress call?" asked Isaac, now hunched over the radio. His back arched over, as he seemed to think he could hear more clearly that way.

"Yes. He said he'd heard music and voices."

This didn't make any sense at all.

"Did he say what the music was or could he tell what language the voices were speaking in?" Isaac felt something cold close around his heart; a tight grip that held him fast.

"He said that it sounded like dance hall music and that he thought that the voices were speaking in English."

"Was it a distress call though?"

"Unknown." Tom signed off.

Isaac sat back down in his chair and looked at Peter. His mind recalled the drum beats he had heard on the short wave radio before. His heart beat faster.

"What does that mean?" asked Peter.

Isaac picked up his glass, finished the dregs and said, "There was no ship."

"What? So what were the signals they were picking up and what about the music, the voices?"

Isaac poured himself another large glass and sat forward.

"You saw something today, in the glass upstairs? What was it?"

Peter looked down into his almost empty glass.

"Something," he whispered.

"A reflection?" asked Isaac.

Peter looked up.

"Yes," he replied. "You've seen it too, haven't you?"

The older man nodded and took a sip.

"Yes. I've seen it as well. I saw it reach out from the glass today. It was trying to grab you when I saw you fall. It appeared to stop when I came around the corner. It was a black smoke-like phantom clawing for your throat. I had seen a reflection in the same glass when I was cleaning it a few months ago. I had my back to the Sun and looked at my reflection, although it wasn't me. Not at first."

"What was it?"

"A ghost, an apparition, I don't know. I think it has something to do with my dream or maybe the dream has something to do with the lighthouse. I just don't know." Isaac sighed and sat back in his chair.

Peter poured himself another drink of whiskey, sat back and closed his eyes.

"That ghoul frightened the hell out of me. I heard a whisper from the shadow but I couldn't make much out of it. I'm sorry I didn't say anything to you, but I thought it was just a trick of the Sun. It blinded me at first and then I looked at the window and thought it was just a black spot from looking at the Sun. Its voice sounded like a hissing sound. I'm sure it said your name."

Isaac looked up. His face wet with tears. He held his head in his hands and wiped his face dry.

"There is something going on in these waters. I've seen things and heard things. In my dream…" he paused.

"The thing in my dream called my name. It hissed and spat my name at me." Isaac wiped his face and stood up. "I still have a job to do here. I need to check on the light and override the fog horn." Isaac began to stand.

"I'll come with you if you're ready" said Peter rising from his seat. Isaac put one hand on his shoulder and pressed him back down.

"It'll take five minutes, that's all."

Isaac looked out of the window. What did George hear, thought Isaac.

Isaac made the checks to the lighthouse and his head started to feel weak. The whiskey was flowing through him, and he needed to sit down. He had checked the lantern and saw that its beam was fanning out to sea, lighting up the black ocean and it peaks and troughs. Its beam steadied itself after three cycles and fixed itself on a point out at sea. Isaac followed its path and saw the waves drive towards the coast line. The clouds still hung in the sky, moving swiftly away parting only to allow the light of the moon to break through and shimmer on the crests. No other life out there. No ships or boats or life boat. It was up to the lighthouse to light the way for any traveller tonight. Five vessels were due to make their way across the safe jurisdiction of the lighthouse after midnight. It was now eleven fifteen. Forty five minutes until the witching hour. Isaac felt tired and weak but vowed to stay awake tonight to ensure he could watch out for every ship that passed his way.

Isaac went back downstairs to find Peter asleep. He pulled out the blankets from Peter's duffel bag and laid them over him. The whiskey glass lay empty on the floor so he picked it up and walked over to the kitchen area. He boiled the kettle and made a large mug of black coffee. He took it over to the radio and contacted the coast guard again. Tom informed him that that the helicopter would be back tonight, patrolling the night sky. The weather had started to ease now and visibility was returning to normal. He finished off the coffee quickly and put the mug into the sink. He needed some fresh air so moved around to the door and quietly opened it. Putting on his thick waterproof he stepped out into the night. He held onto the rail surrounding the lighthouse tower with his flash light hung from his left hand. He moved himself around to the east of the tower looking out to sea and took deep breathes into his lungs. It was then he noticed the wood strewn over the rocks at the base of the lighthouse. With a tight grip on the rail, he swung the flash light over the wreckage. His heart pounded in his chest, threatening to burst out at any moment. He couldn't make out much detail so moved around to the boat house where a boat hook was soundly fastened to the building. He carefully took out his keys and unlocked the pad lock which kept the hook in place. Lifting it out of its cradle Isaac held it in his left hand and passed the flash light to his right. He gradually made his way back to the debris. He leaned back against the lighthouse wall, shone the light onto some of the wood bobbing about nearby and stretched the hook out to try and catch hold of a piece. He struggled to get a decent hold of anything and feared that he may lose his balance. The weather began to turn and clouds started to form over the bay. The wind blew across the sea and waves started to disturb the wood as he struggled to get hold of anything. His hair caught up in the fresh breeze and flicked at his eyes. Finally, the hook snatched onto a long piece of wood and Isaac guided it over the rocks. He moved it around to the right and it dropped to the path. Steadily, he made his way around then bent down. Examining the wood confirmed his fears. This was what remained of The Lizzie. Waves began to crash into the rocks with more force as he decided to get back inside. Moving around to the left would give him the shortest route back to the door. Another wave hit the rocks sending fresh white spray around his back. He was almost at the door when a huge wave struck him knocking him to the path with such gusto that he lost hold of the boat hook and the flash light. They both lodged in the rocks as he tried to gain his footing. The flash light's beam pointed up and straight into his face, temporarily blinding him. The weight of the wave still felt to be there as he tried to stand. He slipped to one side and the burnt remains of the corpse slumped to the floor. Isaac scrambled away around the path backing away with his hands behind him and his legs kicking out furiously. The black scorched body contorted itself into a grotesque pose. Its arms were bent and its fingers fixed into a set of claws. Isaac took quick gasps of air as another wave hit the rocks moving the dead body closer to him He frantically grabbed for the light behind him on the rocks. His fingers wrapped around the torch on and swept it back to focus on the body. Flaps of burnt clothes made the corpse look like it had loose skin flapping in the wind. Isaac knew he had to get it inside but whoever it was, it was one of the lifeboat men and Peter's friend. It lay on its back staring blankly into the night sky. He couldn't risk Peter seeing this dreadful sight. The boat house! Isaac had to get the corpse into his boat locked up in the boat house. That meant that he had to move the corpse back through the waves and unlock the boat house whilst holding onto the hook and the flash light. First, get the hook, he thought. He managed to locate the hook stuck between two large rocks then moved back towards the dead sailor. He managed to lift the body closer to the lighthouse wall to protect it from the attack of those sinister waves. For some reason, he then thought of the time. He looked at his watch as the hands showed twelve o'clock. Midnight! "Right!" he said aloud. Moving as swiftly as he could, he managed to make his way back to the boathouse and dropped the hook back into its home. Now with a free hand he unlocked the door as both boats rose and fell with the swell of the oncoming waves. The door faced the coast line so access to the boats was easier than it could have been. He then retrieved the hook and brought his own boat out of the shed. The wooden pole had a hook fastened on both ends so he attached one to the boat and brought it round to the safer side of the lighthouse away from any rogue waves. The other end he then hooked onto the rail where it would hold for just enough time for Isaac to move the body into the small boat. Knowing that he was running out of time and energy he went back for the body and lifted it over his shoulder. Each step he took drained so much of his strength that he thought that he'd lose the fight and fall only to be taken into the callous black sea. The effort was getting too much for Isaac. The moon broke the clouds briefly and lit up the grisly scene as he crept back to the boat. He looked like Burke or Hare in their body-snatching days. Finally, he made it to the boat and hoisted the dead man into it. Bringing the cover over its cargo he unloosened the hook from the rail and pushed the boat back into its home. Exhausted, he locked the boat house and made the short journey back around to the door and to the safety of the lighthouse.

Stepping back inside, he locked the door and slid down it. His eyes winced at the light in the room and he heard Peter snoring in the chair. He needed to let the coast guard head quarters know that he had found a body but all his strength had gone. As he tried to stand he lost the fight and slipped into unconsciousness on the floor.

"Isaac."

That voice again.

"Isaac." It came again.

"No...what!" yelled Isaac as his eyes opened to see Peter leaning over him, shaking his shoulders.

"Isaac. Come on. You're fine, you're awake now."

Peter helped Isaac to the chair and he slumped into it heavily.

Peter had woken up to find Isaac in a crumpled heap on the floor and he'd thought the worst.

"Are you okay, Isaac?"

Groggily, Isaac looked up to see the concern on Peter's face.

"Do I look that bad?"

"Well, you've looked better. I'll get you a drink." Peter left his side and fetched a tall glass of cold water.

Isaac drank it down and sat up. His mind was starting to piece together the events from the previous night. He went through the evening in his head, remembering the storm and the wind. A vision of a great flash appeared in his brain opening up the pain of seeing the life boat engulfed in flames. The body! Oh no! The dead body of one of the crew was stored in the boat house.

"What time is it?"

"Just gone five."

"Peter. Sit down. I found something last night. The life boat was wrecked outside the lighthouse. Broken and burnt wood was being washed up by the storm. I found a body."

Peter sat in stunned silence.

"I don't know who it is, but we need to contact the coast guard now and have them collect him."

Peter hung his head. Isaac walked over to him and placed a friendly hand on his shoulder.

"We need to go to the boat house. That's where I stored him. It was rough out there last night. I thought it best to move him into my boat to make sure he'd be safe."

"Let me see," said Peter, raising his head to look up at Isaac.

"I might be able to identify him."

"He was badly burnt, Pete. I won't be easy for you to see."

Peter stood up and put on his coat and went to the door.

Isaac followed, unlocked the door and they stepped out into the morning air. The sea was calm and the white clouds wandered aimlessly on their way. The pair moved slowly around to the front of the lighthouse, delaying the prospect of seeing the dead friend of Peter. Seagulls played across in the bay. They carried on their usually daily routine as though the world was always the same as it had been. But it had changed. It had changed for Peter and it had changed for Isaac. As they neared the boat house, Isaac noticed something very odd. The wood had gone. It could have loosened itself from the rocks and drifted ashore, but not all of it. Peter glanced at him and asked him the same thing that his brain was trying to work out, "Where's the wood?"

"I don't know." He took the keys out of his pocket and unlocked padlock for the hook then the door to the boat house. Both boats rocked gently in their small shed. He hooked his boat and withdrew it from the house and pulled into the jetty behind the lighthouse where he had dealt with the dreadful chore last night.

They both took hold of the boat and Isaac pulled back the cover. It was empty but for a few tools and the oars. Isaac stared at the boat. His mouth opened but no sound came out. He turned to look at Peter.

"Where is he?"

Isaac looked back into the boat and shook his head.

"I don't understand." Isaac stepped into the boat and felt the floor. There was no sign of any of the water that had accompanied the body he had placed in there less than six hours previously. It was a little damp but nowhere near as wet as it would have been if a body that had been dragged from the sea had been stowed in there.

"Is there any way you put the body in my boat?" Peter asked.

"We need to check, I was tired and I'd had a few whiskeys last night. I suppose it's possible."

They moved back around to the boat house and hooked Peter's boat. Bringing it around to the jetty, they looked at each other. Peter's face looked stern and cold. He had doubts about Isaac's story.

"I know what I did last night, Pete. My coat is still damp from last night and look at my shoulder."

A dark stain covered his right shoulder where he remembered lifting the charred corpse last night. Peter looked at his coat and could clearly see what looked like charcoal had discoloured a section of the cloth.

They pulled Pete's boat ashore and checked it from bow to stern. Only Peter's tools, diesel and a few boxes lay in the boat.

"What's going on?" said Peter.

After they had moored both boats safely, they returned to the lighthouse.

"Call the coast guard" said Peter. "Let's get all the facts."

It made sense, but he had spoken to them last night and knew that only two bodies had been recovered. Four bodies were still out there and he knew in his heart that he had found one last night. Even if it hadn't been a body, maybe a broken piece of wood, then it would still have been in his boat; at the very least, in Pete's boat. But it was a body.

Isaac sat by the radio and called the coast guard, Tom. After five minutes speaking to him he had it confirmed that the boat had been struck by lightning and all the crew had been lost. They had recovered two bodies that were now lying in a mortuary room at Scarborough hospital. The other four had yet to be found. It was suspected that they would eventually been washed up somewhere down the coast.

Isaac thanked Tom and asked for his condolences to be passed onto the families.

Peter sat staring at Isaac.

"How could you have been wrong? It's not something you make a mistake about."

"I found a body, Pete. As I made my way back around to come inside, I was struck by what I thought was just a wave. As I tried to move, the body fell off my back and I scrambled away. I was in shock, but I know what I saw." Isaac felt agitated and yet so helpless.

What had happened out there? How could he think that he had moved a body into a boat when he quite apparently hadn't?

Peter sat still. "Okay, Isaac. You've been having a really bad time lately. You need a break from this lighthouse. Come and stay with me and Sally. She'll make up an extra bed for you and she's a good cook."

Isaac considered it briefly.

"Thanks, Pete, but I can't leave here. I've got to make sure that this lighthouse does what it is meant to do. I've got to keep the place going. I know its quirks and what it needs. It needs me and I need it. I hope you understand."

"I know you think you're doing the right thing, but the offer stands. Anytime."

"Thank you, Peter. Look, make yourself something to eat. I'm going to get ready."

Isaac needed to get out of his clothes. He made his way to the bathroom and drew a bath. While the bath filled, he decided to rid himself of the grey beard he was now sporting. Peter was right, he did need a break, but how could he leave here? Last night's heartbreaking events only cemented the idea that he had to stay and do his job. The man in the mirror looked back at him with sad eyes; dark rings encircling them. As he washed his face and applied the shaving foam, he noticed a contusion on his right shoulder. He half turned his body so he could see his back. Purple bruises marked his shoulder and upper back. He wiped away the foam with the towel and reached his left arm round and touched one of them. He winced at his own touch. The wave on its own could not have made such a mess, he thought. Something hit me. Then he gently slipped into the hot bath. The water felt good on his body until it touched his back. He gave out a deep grunt as it stung his injuries. As the feeling subsided, he slowly settled into the bath.

CHAPTER FIVE

The noise becomes silent

A blanket to hold

No eyes or ears

The monster breaks free

Isaac never knew his father, William Isaac Shepherd. His paternal grandparents had both died long before he was born and he knew nothing about them. His mother's parents were both still alive but too ill to attend his wedding. Alice looked radiant and Isaac wore his war medals with pride.

Isaac did his duty and served his time in the Royal Navy. For almost six years, he fought alongside his fellow sailors. Much of the time, he would spend in the vast engine room ensuring that the huge battleship would continue to run and help in the war effort. An engineer by trade and a very good one at that. In 1941, he was transferred to a new ship and was called upon to fight in what would be known as the Battle of Cape Matapan, against the Italian navy. The Royal Navy were joined by several warships of the Australian Navy. His ship, the HMS Hotspur was a destroyer built back in the mid 1930s and had seen many battles in the Spanish Civil War. The plucky vessel had been badly damaged and was repaired in a shipyard in Malta. It was fully repaired and ready for battle when Isaac joined the crew. After the success in Greece and the Battle of Cape Matapan, the ship was then transferred to the Eastern Fleet. He wanted to stay with the ship, but in 1940 it was called back into dry-dock for a major refit. Isaac was then transferred to another ship, the mighty HMS Warspite where he served for four years. This huge warship played a pivotal role in Operation Neptune on June the 6th 1944 giving covering fire for the brave soldiers who faced insurmountable odds. The Normandy Landings assault proved to be one of the most important operations of the Second World War. Over one hundred and fifty thousand allied troops descending on the beaches with a loss of almost twelve thousand. Isaac's pride in that ship and the Royal Navy would never leave him and his heart ached when he had to leave the HMS Warspite and join his final commission; the HMS Valour. His Navy life finished with a tour of the Atlantic.

The raucous sounds of rock 'n roll was the new passion for his young wife. She had met some American GI's during their time in England and found their company exciting. Her head was turned. They had introduced her to new things she had no idea even existed; music, fun, freedom and sex. This proved to be an enticing time for Alice and she intended to make the most out of it. She didn't know if her new husband would return from war. His letters had stopped and no news came from him. She would dream of his death night after night. She would wake and cry out in the middle of the night for him but when she reached over to see another American GI laying next to her, she new in her heart that he was dead.

After Isaac left the Royal Navy on the 26th of July 1945, the same day his beloved HMS Valour was broken up and turned into scrap. Alice couldn't believe that he had survived. His letters had not made it back home. As soon as her saw her, his heart broke in two. He could sense that things had changed but he was a proud man. For the next twelve years, he tried to settle into married life with Alice. His time in the war left him wanting to stay at home and enjoy the local wildlife and calming classical music. The traumatic scenes he had witnessed only served to make Isaac want peace. Peace for himself and peace for the World. Alice wanted more than Isaac could or would offer her. For those years, Isaac tried, but deep down he knew it was not enough. He couldn't live with the New Britain after the war and Isaac and Alice drifted further apart.

Alice and Isaac tried to make a home together, but even at the very early stage of their marriage they both knew that something wasn't right. Alice was very keen to go out with her friends to dance the night away. Isaac could see that she was having her fun and could see how happy she was when she met up with them. The only problem was that she wasn't happy with him. After the years he had spent at sea in the Navy, Isaac needed to feel settled down.

Isaac tried to find work, but it had proved very difficult. Alice's father owned a textile firm in West Yorkshire and offered Isaac a position in the weaving shed. It was dirty and noisy, but with his experience in the Navy working as an engineer he managed to be useful fixing the old weaving looms. The huge warehouse contained almost one hundred looms which slogged away day in day out to produce cloth and fine fabrics for suits and other materials. The wood and metal shuttles would fly across the loom back and forth at very high speeds. Occasionally, a shuttle could break and would be shot out through the end of the loom. Some unfortunate weaver could be hit by these flying missiles and injuries could be fatal. It was not unheard of for a weaver to be struck in the eye. The managers, or "overlookers" would need to ensure the smooth running of these mammoth machines and would have the know-how to get the looms back on track. Isaac worked alongside them as constant maintenance was required. They were allowed to live in one of her father's many houses. It was small and uncomfortable but at least they had somewhere to live and he had a job. Their one bedroom was sparse save for a wardrobe, his father's chest-of-drawers and their cold double bed. Isaac had few clothes and wore his work clothes most of the time. He had the suit that he married Alice, a cream shirt, brown tie and brown brogues. He paid her father a modest rent for them to live there although Alice spent her time between her parents' home and their house. As a wedding present, her parents had given them a puppy border collie. His mainly white coat was marred by a grey black smudge on his left flank and a black stripe down his face. They named him Steam. Their small house wasn't big enough for them let alone a dog as well so Alice would take him with her on her daily visits to see her mother. Steam spent a lot of time with his surrogate family.

Isaac stuck at the job for almost twelve years, but in that time he and Alice saw very little of each other and had begun to grow even further apart. Isaac was always tired after his long shift at the weaving shed. Alice would go out on a Saturday night with two of her friends, Anne and Maggie. They would go dancing in the new dance halls which had started to spring up all over the country. As American music spread through the halls, more risqué dancing followed. Rock 'n roll was here to stay. Alice remembered her time during the latter part of the war and the two GI's she had met back then. Bud and Joe had shown her a good time and she longed for those feelings again. Isaac had no time for the modern music and shunned those places. He knew that Alice had to have some fun with her friends but didn't realise just how much she was having. On some nights she would say that she would stay with Anne or Maggie overnight as the buses back home from Leeds didn't feel safe. He found himself fetching her from her friends' house on the Sunday morning and bringing her back home by bus. She would fall asleep on his shoulder as the bus rattled its way back to their home. He would look down at her dainty hands and gently smooth them with his callused, worn hands. His heart felt heavy and he managed to sniff away a tear on more than one occasion.

On one particular Sunday, he had turned up a little early at Maggie's home to find that Alice was not there. As he waited, Alice came rushing into the house shouting to Maggie about her wonderful night with her new man. Isaac stood up and pushed past her in the hallway. Alice was shocked to see her husband there and ran after him. As she caught up to him he turned to her and said it was over. His heart was split in two.

Now, as he sat in the bath, his thoughts went through the events of the last twenty four hours. How happy he felt when Peter had come to visit. How things had turned sour with Pete's vision and the catastrophic loss of the lifeboat. What of the body he had found? Could he have been mistaken? Was it the even body of one of the missing crew?

After he had bathed, he went through to his bedroom and looked at the photographs set in their individual frames. The middle photo of his wedding day just looked wrong now. Isaac couldn't quite make out what it was, but there was something amiss. He studied the photo and noticed that Alice wasn't looking at the camera. Her gaze seemed distant as though she was looking for some reason as to why she had married at all. It must have always been like that but he just hadn't noticed it.

He went back down to see Peter and found him sitting in the doorway idly watching the seabirds feed. His shoulders were hunched over.

"The bathroom is all yours, Pete." Isaac touched his shoulder.

Peter slowly moved from his chair and wearily wandered through to the bathroom.

"Thanks." Peter didn't turn around. "I'm going to have to go and see the families today, Isaac. I'm sorry, I know I said that I'd stay here tonight, but I really need to do this."

"I understand" said Isaac.

Isaac needed to understand the history of the lighthouse and had decided to contact the largest library in Yorkshire; the York library. Whilst Peter used his bathroom, he radioed through to the coast guard who then connected him through to the operator who in turn patched him through to the library. He spoke to a very helpful woman called Angela.

"I wonder if you could help me. I'm looking for the history of lighthouses on the East coast of Yorkshire."

"Yes sir, we have archive files for Yorkshire and I'm sure we could find what you're looking for," replied Angela.

"Would you have old newspapers in the archive as well?"

"We do. They go back to 1893 when the first library was opened by the Duke and Duchess of York. We also have a section of papers donated by locals that date back before then."

"Would I need to book some time with those at all, Angela."

"Yes, we can arrange a time and a date for you. I can arrange for the appropriate files and papers to be put to one side for you on the day. Of course, some of these papers are very old so you would need to have a supervisor with you. Some of these papers are very rare."

"That's wonderful, Angela. I need to make some arrangements, but I'd like to come over to take a look sometime within the next couple of weeks."

They arranged a date and a time. Angela would prepare the newspapers and find the appropriate books for when Isaac would visit. He needed to have cover for the lighthouse and also to get a train down to York. As it would only be for the day, he thought about asking Peter. He didn't want to burden his friend, but he had to make this journey and Pete was his closest friend. The days were getting longer and he would be back before nightfall.

After a while Peter came back out of the bathroom having shaved and bathed. Isaac had packed Peter's belongings into his bag and stood at the door holding a mug of coffee.

"I'm going to get moving old friend."

"Of course. Look Peter, it may not be the best time to ask, but I'm going to need a favour myself."

Isaac told him about his planned trip to York and the reason for his need. Peter agreed to look after the lighthouse for him.

"Thank you, Isaac" said Peter collecting his bag.

"What for?"

"Being a friend," he said and patted Isaac's right shoulder as he walked past him. They walked together around to the boathouse and Isaac unlocked the wooden structure. They brought out Peter's boat and he leapt aboard. After a couple of tugs on the starter, the boat spluttered into life and Peter turned and gave a salute to his friend. Isaac walked back around to the door and watched Peter's little boat cut through the calm sea. Seabirds swooped down to feed on the fish which had been brought up to the surface by the churning of Pete's motor boat.

Isaac removed the cloth from his easel. The new painting was taking some time to complete. Isaac wasn't happy with it but wanted to see it through to its conclusion. The rocks and cliff face were coming on nicely and the boats looked good. The way he had caught the waves rolling up to the rocks and shimmer in the sunlight as they smashed looked as though they had shattered into a million jewels. That had turned out really well. The sky above showed dark, heavy pendulous clouds looming over the cliff tops. He wasn't happy with the cliff edges. As he tried to sort out the serrated rocks littered with heather and other foliage, his knife cut deep into the picture and dragged straight across the painting. The dark red wound bled across the picture from top right to bottom left. Isaac watched his own hand ruin the painting. The knife twisted in his hand and he put more pressure on the canvas until it ripped under the knife's assault. Red paint surged out of the wound and covered the painting. He dropped the knife which clattered to the floor and kicked the easel over. He felt angry and scared at the same time. What was happening to him? He picked up the easel and examined the picture to check the damage. The painting was undamaged and whole. No cut and no red line. He studied the picture and could see no sign of the vicious attack he had just made. He placed it on the floor and slowly stepped away to look at it from a few feet away. The rugged sea at the bottom of the painting seemed to consist of letters. Jagged letters spelt out from left to right "I - S - A - A - C". He couldn't fathom out why he had painted the letters or why the red gash and rip had disappeared. He felt ill and ran to the door to vomit outside. Seagull feeding fled the water with screeches of terror when he lost his breakfast and then his footing. He fell backwards and hit the wall with a sickening thud. He wiped his mouth rubbed his shoulder and stood up. Things were looking very dark to Isaac. He needed to know if there was anything strange about the lighthouse and whether something was showing him these weird visions and giving him nightmares. It had begun to show itself at night and now it seemed during the day. His visit to the library in York couldn't come soon enough for him. The picture lay discarded on the floor as he stepped over to pick it up. The letters had disappeared. His mind felt as though it was breaking up and splintering in his head. He wanted answers to questions that he didn't even know how to ask.

The following week saw the funeral of Peter's dear friends. Many people turned up for the crew and family as friends said their goodbyes. The Flamborough lifeboat team had been assembled and had already begun their new duty of patrolling a much larger area along with the assistance of the Coast Guard's Sea King helicopter. The skipper had worked alongside George in the past and had enough experience to take over the reins. Peter and Isaac stood in the church amongst the many people.

"How are you doing, Pete?" asked Isaac.

"I'm okay," he shrugged.

It was a difficult day for the whole community as young and old stood singing the hymns and the vicar recited his eulogy. The funeral was held for all six men and although only two had been recovered from the ocean, six coffins lay side by side in the church.

"Would you excuse me for a while, Isaac?"

"Of course, I understand."

Peter approached one of the women. She was shrouded in black as were the other wives and she held out her hands to him. Isaac watched from a distance as Peter held her hands tenderly and whispered into her left ear. Her face was obscured by the black veil until she slowly lifted it. Alice stood there, looking into Isaac's eyes. As he stared, her features changed into a woman unrecognisable to him. She lowered her eyes and droplets of diamond like tears rolled softly, silently down her left cheek. She again lowered her veil. The image of his dead wife's face lingered in his mind and he knew that he would never see her again.

A week later, Peter's little boat moored at Thornside lighthouse. Isaac was ready and waiting and jumped aboard his own boat. The motor spluttered then leapt into life. Isaac waved to Pete who saluted back in return. As he looked over his shoulder at the tall white and red lighthouse tower he called home, he realised that he hadn't left it for well over a decade. It looked magnificent to him, a real beacon for the sailors and fishermen traversing these dangerous waters. He felt an emotion welling up inside him as his eyes became wet, though not from the spray of the water. He did love his life out here and knew that he would indeed feel like the proverbial fish out of water when he would arrive in York.

He moored his little boat in the harbour at Scarborough and made his way to the train station. The train left the station on time and it headed off to York. He watched the view out of his window change from town to countryside and from village to rivers. Little villages passed by, fleeting and only for a moment. He saw people going about their daily lives with all of their individual problems. The people went by as quickly as the towns and villages in a brief breath in time. He wondered what their lives held for them and what kind of dreams they had. He then turned his attention back to the reason for his visit and what the future would hold for him.

The train pulled into the magnificent Victorian York train station. Isaac marvelled at the architectural and technical achievement that this station truly inspired. He reached for his bag in the overhead netting and made his way to the train door. Families with children and businessmen mingled together, vying for position in a race to see who could get out first. Isaac stood back and allowed the throng to escape the train. He felt relaxed even though the reason for his trip might bring up information that he really didn't like to know, but knew it was imperative for him to find out. He may find nothing unusual although he had the feeling that he might not be so lucky.

He stepped out into the fresh York morning and headed for the library on Museum Street. The ancient city wall which surrounded the city stood tall and proud. He stared up at it and studied the old grey stones. Each one had seen years of history unfold and of lives passing by. The wall had been here long before his birth and would still stand long after he was gone. Whatever he would find out today would soon be consigned to history like everything that had gone before. He knew that his destiny lay in this medieval city. It was a short walk to the library, just ten minutes. As he approached the magnificent gothic cathedral, the York Minster, the sun lit it up as though it were the most important place on earth. He stood and marvelled at the beautiful building. To his left stood the library.

The imposing building's entrance was flanked by two outstretched arms of brick and glass housing the books and texts within. Two tall stone pillars stood either side of the entrance as Isaac stepped through the doors.

The lush entrance hall only hinted at the multitude of fascinating books held in its illustrious walls. Above the reception desk there was a circular hole which allowed more light from the upper floor, to find its way into the dark building. A pair of staircases wound their way up from either side of the entrance. He walked over to the information desk and introduced himself to the receptionist. Angela shook his hand. "It's a pleasure to meet you Mr. Shepherd." Angela's vice like grip hand shake gave him the assurance that this woman would be able to find any information he required. "Likewise."

"If you'd like to come with me, I've found some books and papers that you might find interesting."

Isaac followed Angela through to a room next to the reception area and unlocked the door. A damp foisty smell met his nose as the door opened. A mixture of mothballs and ancient decay filled his nostrils and he felt light-headed. Angela didn't flinch.

"I've set out the books I think you'll need and will have Arthur bring in the old papers when you are ready. I would ask you not to smoke, eat or drink anything whilst you are in this room. The books are mainly one-of-a-kind and we don't want any accidents. If you need to have a break, please come and see me so that I can lock the room again."

Her formal frostiness belied her youth. Isaac put her in her mid twenties although her manner and clothing indicated and woman forty years her senior. The tight bun of hair on the top of her head seemed to pull her face into cat-like features. She wore little makeup and her skin looked faultless.

"Thank you so much." Isaac entered the room and felt a cold breeze blow onto his neck which chilled him through like the winds of the North Sea.

He settled down in the wooden chair at the old desk. The old chair creaked at his weight and Isaac wondered whether it would be up to the job of keeping his behind off the wooden floor. He hoped so as he didn't like the idea of getting wood splinters ripping through his trousers and digging deep into his flesh. Four books were piled neatly on the left of the desk. A writing pad and pen sat at right angles to the right hand corner of the desk.

"Very efficient," said Isaac.

"Sorry?" asked Angela as she poked her head back through the doorway. He thought she had left.

"Oh, I just said aloud that I should get on now." Isaac felt as though he had been caught swearing by a nun.

"If you need anything else, please come and see me at the front reception."

"Again, thank you" said Isaac as Angela finally left.

The top book was entitled "A Yorkshire History – Volume One" and was dated 1910. As he carefully opened the old book the yellowing paper whispered. He touched its surface and felt the hard abrasive paper beneath his fingers. He scanned the index and found a section regarding lighthouses. In it he read about the Flamborough lighthouse which is still referred to as the "new lighthouse". It was built in 1806 to replace to old beacon which had been built back in 1674. It had cost £8,000 to build and design and was first lit on the 1st of December 1806. It was the first lighthouse to incorporate a red glass in its lantern along with two light ones. His own lighthouse had this very same feature. He took a few notes from the book and then he placed it carefully in the top right hand corner of the desk.

The second book was "Memoir on the Origin and Incorporation of the Trinity House of Deptford Strond" by Joseph Cotton published in 1818. This gave an account of the creation of Trinity House who looked after the welfare of Britain's lighthouses. Amongst the entries there was mention of various parishes such as Whitby, Robin Hood's Bay, Scarbro', Flambro' and Bridlington. It also listed the sizes, colours, names and numbers of all the buoys set in Britain's channels dated May 1818. Detailed accounts were laid out and full information relating to the formation and pensions graced the pages. Interesting reading, thought Isaac, but nothing about Thornside.

The third book dated back to 1901 and was named "Tales of vessels – The Yorkshire Coast 1800 to 1899". He flicked through to the index and found an entry for a Thornwick Lighthouse built in 1786. Gently turning the pages he found the section relating to this lighthouse tower. He found that it had been destroyed in a fire in 1870 due to the failings of its keeper. It had been thought that he had been drinking heavily since a disaster a couple of weeks before whereby a freight vessel had struck a passenger liner. Records showed that all aboard both ship and boat had been lost at sea. The keeper had been found to have been at fault by not lighting the flame on that fateful night of December third 1870. On that night, the Crantock had set sail from Aberdeen to carry its cargo to Rotterdam. The cruise liner Livingstone, sailed the same waters in a terrible storm. As they both approached the bay, no light warned them of the dangers which lay ahead. The lighthouse was home to a keeper who had been sanctioned with the duty to man the beacon and to keep safe the water's travellers. As the storm hit, the keeper failed to light the lantern. A crew member of the liner spotted the cargo ship and set off two fireworks in order to alert both vessels of their proximity to one another. His actions were too late as two hundred and fifty four men, women and children died that night. There was no mention of the keeper's name. Shortly after the disaster a fire swept through the lighthouse and a new one was sanctioned. The old Thornwick Lighthouse was demolished as the fire damage made it unsafe. Two years later, the Thornside Lighthouse opened. The light shone out for the first time on the 1st of December 1872 .Isaac sat back in the chair as it creaked beneath his weight. His lighthouse had replaced the destroyed Thornwick Lighthouse. He feverishly wrote down the details. He needed some fresh air, so went out to the reception to see Angela.

He reached the desk but found no sign of Angela. Instead a young man with shoulder length hair flicked through the rotary filing system.

"Excuse me; do you know where Angela is?" Isaac asked the youth.

"Erm, I think she's gone to see the head librarian. Can I help you at all?"

"I'm doing a little research in the room over there…"

"Ah," the man interrupted, "You're the gentleman scouring the old books about the lighthouses."

"Yes, that's right."

"Angela left me the key for the room should you need a break. I'll lock it up if you want?"

"Thank you. I'm just going to get some fresh air and maybe some food."

"There's a really nice little café just down the road. Cross over here, turn right, then you'll see it to the left. They do some nice things in there," informed the polite young man.

"Lovely. I'll just get my notes before you lock up." He checked his watch. It was just gone eleven o'clock.

As he stepped out into the cool fresh air, he felt as though he was starting to understand a little more about the coast he called home. He crossed over the road then followed the instructions that the receptionist had given him and found the café. It was brightly painted and the smell of fresh coffee wafted out of the door. He found himself a seat and a waitress took his order of coffee and a slice of fruit cake. Taking out his notebook, he flicked through the details he had written therein. The coastline had been protected by light since mid 1600 and he was carrying on the duty over 300 years later. He wondered just how many ships had been saved in that time. Or, more to the point, how many had been lost. The waitress brought over his coffee and placed a china plate before him with a moist looking piece of homemade fruit cake.

"Thank you," he said without looking up.

"You're welcome, I'm sure," said the disembodied voice.

I need to find out the name of the keeper, he thought to himself. Maybe I could trace his family tree. He paid for his snack and returned to the library.

He saw the young man stood behind the reception desk speaking to a young girl of about eighteen. The man was obviously attracted to her as he chatted away in a very peculiar and animated way. He appeared to be dancing, waving his arms in the air, until he spotted Isaac. Stuttering and stammering he tried to regain his composure and leaned closely to the young girl. She giggled and pushed him away then coyly turned her head round to peek at Isaac standing by the door. Her long brown hair wafted gently around her shoulders as she turned and Isaac could just see her eyes with long dark eyelashes protecting them from above. She bit her lip and laughed.

"Sorry sir," the young man said.

"That's fine," he said. He recognised what young love looked like and envied them. Would he ever be in that position again? He strongly doubted it.

"Did you find the café sir?" He had managed to stop blushing now, but still looked a little flustered. The young girl turned to face Isaac and placed her elbows on the desk behind her. She wore a long flowery dress and floppy hat.

"Thank you, I did. Can I get back into the room please?"

"Yes, of course sir. Can you just give me a moment?"

He reached over the desk and touched his girlfriend's arm. She turned and kissed him full on the lips, turned, walked past Isaac and brushed against the old man's arm.

"Nice girl," he said to the young man.

"My girlfriend, Alice."

Her name again. Would it haunt him forever?

They walked down the corridor and saw Angela walking toward him. Angela greeted him at the door.

"How is your research going, Mr. Shepherd?" she enquired.

"Well, very well thank you. I wondered, would it be possible to have a look at those old newspapers now?"

"Certainly sir. I'll ask Arthur to bring them in for you. I made a selection for you. I hope there are going to be of use."

"I do hope so." Isaac went on. "You said that you had some papers donated to the library dating back some years before it opened?"

"Yes, we have a number of those, but as I said, they are very rare and somewhat faded now."

"I'm really after a specific date. The 4th of December 1870."

"Let me see for you."

After what seemed like an eternity, Angela came to the room with, who Isaac assumed to be Arthur in tow. Arthur followed Angela with his head bowed down in a very subservient manner. By doing so, Isaac could see that the old man had a very prominent bald patch surrounded by fair wispy hair. As he approached, Arthur looked up with sad watery pale blue eyes. Puffy bags hung loosely beneath them. Bloated jowls hung down either side of his face. He resembled a Basset Hound. "Poor chap" thought Isaac.

Angela broke his train of thought.

"Apparently, the 4th of December was a Sunday and we have no paper for that date. Very few were printed on Sundays. I have found a newspaper from the 5th which may suit your needs."

"Wonderful, thank you."

Arthur settled down the papers. His white gloved hands caressed the old parchment.

"Arthur will turn the pages for you, and I ask you not to sneeze on them. Thank you." Angela's stern demeanour left Isaac feeling uncomfortable.

Arthur shuffled next to Isaac a little too close for his comfort.

"Now then sir, these are very valuable pieces of history we have in front of us. I shall turn the pages when you are ready. Please resist the temptation to touch them."

Arthur seemed to be like a Charles Dickens character. He almost expected him to say "Ever so humble sir" in a very Uriah Heap kind of way. His cheeks wobbled with each phrase.

There were a number of newspapers on the table. The top one, Northern Echo had the sections "The War News," "General Markets" and "Shipping Intelligence". The Darlington paper had only started publishing from the beginning of 1870. The headlines were of the Franco-Prussian war. He asked Arthur to turn to the next page. Amongst the articles, Isaac focused on the one headlined "Aberdeen Vessel sinks Liner". He learned forward to inspect the print.

"Not too close, please sir." Arthur put his arm across Isaac's chest.

"I need to be able to read it, Arthur," he insisted.

Reluctantly, Arthur withdrew his arm.

As he leaned in, Isaac read the following:

"On the evening of the third day of December 1870, the haulage vessel Crantock struck the liner, The Livingstone sinking both vessels. The Crantock had left Aberdeen harbour earlier in the day and had set sail for Rotterdam. The liner, its bow breached, sank with all hands…" Isaac moved on, scanning for a name.

"The lighthouse keeper, one Isaac Shepherd, had neglected to light the fire in the lighthouse which would have warned The Livingstone of the approaching vessel. Visibility was reported to have been very poor that night with high winds and rain." Isaac froze and stared at the name. Isaac Shepherd. He searched through his memory for his family members. His father had died in 1918 and his grandfather, Tobias Shepherd had died in 1910. He knew that his Great Grandfather had been the black sheep of the family and nobody had told him much about him. So, he shared the name of his Great Grandfather.

"Do you have any more newspapers around this time?" he asked of Arthur.

"We have a number of newspapers following this one, yes sir."

Arthur steadily took the paper he was reading, and gently placed it out of harm's way.

He fumbled through the other papers and brought out four which covered the period over the next month.

One by one, they scoured through them until they found another news story.

"Lighthouse keeper dies after fire."

The newspaper was dated two weeks after the first story.

"It has been reported that the keeper who failed to set alight the flame at Thornwick Lighthouse on the North Yorkshire coast which resulted in the loss of two hundred and fifty four lives, has himself now died after a fire at the lighthouse. It is believed that his lungs had been damaged by the fire and he succumbed six days later. He leaves behind him a wife, Betty Shepherd."

Isaac leaned back in the chair. It was his Great Grandfather. He was living in the lighthouse which replaced the old one which had been razed to the ground be his own flesh and blood. This had all happened one hundred years ago. The loss of all those souls had been down to one man's ineptitude. That man was his Great Grandfather. He felt sick to his stomach.

"Thank you Arthur, this has all been very useful," he said distantly.

There was no mention of his Grandfather, Tobias.

"Would have any books showing the register of births for the next few months after this date?"

"I'll check for you sir," and Arthur left.

Left alone with his thoughts, Isaac wondered when his Grandfather had been born. It can't have been too long after the fire.

"Here we are sir, we have one dated 1871." Arthur placed a bundle of the table in front of Isaac.

He quickly scanned through the register and soon came across the name Tobias Sheppard, his Grandfather. Born September 2nd, 1871, just less than nine months after his great Grandfather had died.

"Sir, sir are you alright?" Arthur asked quietly.

"Yes, I need to go now." Isaac stood up, gathered the writing pad and his bag, and walked out of the room.

"Did you find what you were looking for Mr. Shepherd?" called Angela from behind the mahogany desk.

"Thank you, I did. You've been very kind. Can I leave a donation for the library?" as he brought out a pound note from his wallet.

"That would be very good of you, sir. Thank you," Angela said and she pointed to a wooden box marked "All donations are very welcome." Isaac dropped the note into the box and walked out of the library.

He walked towards the station not really noticing his surroundings. It was now almost a quarter to four and his train was due to leave York at five fifteen. The short walk would not take more than ten minutes. As he wandered down to Station Road, his mind was working frantically to put some sense into what he had found out at the library. He'd have to contact Trinity House to get confirmation of this information as they would hold records for both his and the previous Thornwick Lighthouse. He could have done that without this trip but he might not have found out about the loss of the vessels. His family history had been tarnished by the episode one hundred years ago. His mother would have known about it when he had first been offered the job of lighthouse keeper. Why couldn't she have told him? It was a little late in the day for any repercussions from what had happened. What difference would it have made had he known about his Great Grandfather? No-one had been forthcoming with any stories about him. Now he knew why.

He entered the station just as it started to rain. He showed his ticket to the inspector and sat on one of the platform seats. The train was already in, but he wanted to sit a while before taking his seat. Was there a remnant or echo from those events a century ago embedded in the lighthouse walls? Did his Great Grandfather's spirit haunt the building? Was the reflection he saw that of his old ancestor? Whose body was washed up on the rocks the night of the life boats demise? He had so many questions and knew nobody who would be able to give him those answers. The guard on the platform shouted that the train would be departing in five minutes and could all those travelling please take their seats. Isaac picked up his bag and climbed the three steps up and onto the carriage. He found his seat and sat down. As the train rumbled slowly out of the station, Isaac took out his note pad began to write:

Isaac Shepherd - born 1917, 53 years old

Father - William Isaac Shepherd born 1895 died 1918, 23 years old

Grandfather - Tobias Shepherd born 1871 – died 1910, 39 years old

Great Grandfather Isaac Shepherd born ? – died 1870, ? years old
He sat back in his seat and closed his eyes.

The rain came in the afternoon. Peter stood in the lantern room overlooking the sea. The rain lashed the glass and the Sun shone from behind him flashing a brilliant white light. He could make out a yacht in the distance and could see the sails blow wildly around the mast, threatening to snap it in two. The sea battled with the yacht tossing it high. Peter reached for Isaac's binoculars and clamped them tightly to his eyes and watched as the fragile white and blue craft fought to stay afloat. The fight didn't take long as the sea claimed the small wooden yacht. The mast fell and the sails dropped into the sea flapping like a fish suddenly fighting for breath. Peter put the binoculars back down onto the chair and turned to make his way down through the lighthouse to call the coast guard. As he knelt to open the hatch in the floor, a dark shadow blocked out the light. The air in the lantern room felt suddenly cold and Peter felt an oppressive cloak cover him. He looked up to see a huge hand reaching out from the blue sky. Its long fingers reached out to the lighthouse. He struggled to get the hatch open but was too slow. The hand smashed through the glass and made a grasp for him. Glass rained down on him as the gigantic hand grabbed him and lifted him out of the safety of the lighthouse's lantern room. He was suspended in the air with wind and rain attacking his body. A chain of skulls was tightly wrapped around the wrist of the massive limb. The thick anchor chain dug deep into the skin and cut black lines around the bloody red arm. The skulls laughed and shrieked as he struggled to free himself from the grasp. A deep evil laugh rang out above him as he looked up to see the face staring down at him out of the black rain clouds. Bright red eyes surrounded by a mane of fire looked into his soul and his heart tightened beneath his painful ribs. Smoke shot out of its nostrils with the noise and force of a hurricane. Peter's hair turned white and his face burned black and red. The hand lifted him higher and higher as he saw the remains of the yacht rise out of the sea. Seaweed trailed behind it as it rose toward him. Screams from the crew scythed through the air and made his ears bleed. The voice of the treacherous head howled with glee as it threw the yacht through the air in a blazing trail across the sky. The crew bawled in terror and pain as their skin melted away revealing flesh and bone. The flesh soon boiled away leaving white bony skeletons. Peter looked on in horror as the face turned to him…"Qui interfecit!" it shrieked as Peter was thrown back down towards the lighthouse. "Murderer!" His weak body struck the tower and blood and bones soaked the white exterior of the lighthouse leaving a red sash of gore.

Isaac jumped in his seat as the inspector shook him awake. "Sir, sir, you're scaring the other passengers." He looked around the carriage to see the faces on the passengers. He saw look the look of disgust and fear at his antics. He had been shouting and thrashing about in his seat when the guard was called. The inspector and the train guard looked down at him.

"Are you alright sir?" asked the guard.

"I'm so sorry; I must have had a nightmare. I'm sorry," he said addressing the rest of the frightened faces around him.

He felt his forehead and found that it was covered in sweat. He took out a clean handkerchief and wiped his face.

"I am sorry," he said seeing the young mother cradling her little boy who looked up at him from beneath her coat with eyes wide.

"We're just coming into Scarborough sir."

He reached for his bag and put on his coat. He wanted to get back to the lighthouse as soon as possible to make sure that Peter was alright.

The train arrived dead on time and this time it was Isaac who rushed for the door. He quickly made his way off the train and showed his ticket to the waiting inspector. His boat was waiting for him in the harbour and ran almost all of the way there. Breathing heavily, Isaac stepped into the little boat and tried to start the motor. It coughed and spluttered but would not start.

"Come on," Isaac pleaded as he pulled the starter cable again.

The engine juddered then stopped.

Isaac closed his eyes and took a deep breath.

"Please, come on." He pulled a third time and this time the engine coughed, spluttered, juddered and came to life. Isaac steadied himself then he carefully guided the small craft safely out of the harbour walls and into the open sea. His mind raced through what he had learned today and also to his disturbing dream. His Great Grandfather had been at the same place one hundred years ago and was responsible for all of those deaths. Was a phantom at work now taking away his friend?

He manoeuvred his boat around the coast line and into his bay. The lighthouse looked as it had done when he had left earlier in the day although he could see no sign of life. He steered the craft up to the rear of the tower and moored his boat there next to Pete's. He tied if off and jumped out of the boat and round to the door. It was wide open when the got there. Stepping inside he called for Peter.

"Pete. Pete!" he shouted.

From high up in the tower he heard his reply.

"I'm up here Isaac. Good trip?" Peter sounded cheery.

Isaac bent over and placed his hands on his knees and breathed deeply. He was getting old. Old and out of breath.

"Yes," he tried to shout, but it just came out as a faint whisper. He coughed and tried again.

"Yes, very interesting," Isaac managed.

Peter came down the stairs wiping his hands clean with a once white cloth.

"I've washed the windows of the lantern, inside and out, the fog horn has been tested and I have four bottles of beer chilling in the fridge. So, it went well, then?"

Isaac motioned to him to sit down. He had started to breathe a little more steady now and then he began.

"I found out a little more than I expected. This lighthouse, well, actually the one that this one replaced was run by my Great Grandfather, Isaac Shepherd."

"No? Really. That's amazing. You knew nothing about your ancestors then you find this."

"It gets worse."

Isaac told Peter the full details but not his dream or fears.

Peter sat back in his chair.

"Well, I'd say your trip was worthwhile then. So what now?" asked Peter.

"I know what happened is ancient history now. There's nothing I can do to change that."

"And the dreams you had?"

"Dreams, that's all."

"What about the time in the lantern room. I saw something and so did you."

Isaac didn't want to tell his friend exactly what he thought it was. That his Great Grandfather was reaching out from beyond the grave to take more lives? That had happened to him just the once and also to his friend. He really hoped that it wouldn't happen again.

"I can't explain that. Maybe it was a trick of the sunlight or just the heat building up in the lantern room. The ventilator was closed so it had got pretty warm in there."

Peter wasn't sure about that but let his line of questioning go and turned to more pressing news.

"Time for a beer, old friend?" he said moving towards the fridge. "All the chores are done. We just need to eat and watch out for any ghosts." He gave Isaac a sly look and smiled.

Isaac returned the smile but felt uneasy.

It was six thirty. They had eaten and had each finished one of the bottles of beer.

"How was the shipping traffic today?" Isaac asked.

"Oh, fairly quiet. A couple of fishing boats came past this morning and a yacht tried its luck this afternoon."

Isaac shifted uneasily in his chair.

"A yacht?"

"Yes, white and blue she was. It looked like a nice little craft. It struggled on across from north to south. I watched it a while through your binoculars."

Should I tell him of my dream on the train, thought Isaac? No, that won't achieve anything he decided. Was it just a coincidence? Yachts have sailed though here many times, so why should that surprise me?

"I'll stay over tonight if you want?" said Peter.

"No, Sally will be expecting you home. I'll be fine. I feel like I have turned a corner in my life, Pete. You get off to your wife."

"If you're sure, then alright."

Isaac saw his friend pilot his boat out and watched as it disappeared around the southern coast line of the bay. It was a clear night and he looked up at the billion pin pricks of light shine down out of the black and blue night sky. The stars looked stunning tonight, he thought. The moon passed slowly over its nightly domain and brought a peace and calmness to the waters. The small waves made a gentle, trickling sound as they smoothly made their way into the bay behind stopping momentarily at the rocks of the lighthouse to leave their greetings. The lighthouse brought its own light to the proceedings as it continuously bathed the cliffs and dark sea with life. He stood watching the display of the moon the stars and lighthouse matching each other with the beauty they gave to the night. He looked at the lighthouse towering above him. It was his and he belonged here. He felt that he also belonged to the lighthouse now. As he looked up, he thought of his Grandfather staring up into the same patch of space and at the same stars. He shuddered at the thought. Even though his ancestor's actions had lead to the death of all those people, he now felt it was his duty to make sure that wouldn't happen again. He would be even more vigilant than he had ever been before.

CHAPTER SIX

Too few to say

Two flew away

Three came again

Their faces gone

Isaac and Alice parted ways in 1957 and divorced one year later. Alice was then free to marry her new beau, a musician in one of the those up-and-coming guitar based rock 'n roll combos. With his slick back hair and drainpipe trousers, Jake had turned her head and relit her libido. At thirty six, she was still very pretty and petite. Isaac always looked at her as though she were a porcelain doll who needed pretty clothes and a good brush of her hair. Alice was not a shrinking violet though, and she felt smothered by Isaac who she saw as an old man even though he was only forty three years old. He was very old fashioned with his ideas and found it difficult to change for her. Jake was only too happy to indulge in his fantasies with Alice.

At six foot two, he towered above Alice in much the same way as Isaac had done. However, that is where the resemblance between the started and ended. Jake's jet black sleek hair was combed into a fashionable DA. His hair protruded forth over his head in a dark wave of a quiff, shielding his blue eyes from the overhead Sun. The collar of his leather jacket touched the base of his hair and framed his features with a black sheen. A white sleeveless t-shirt covered his taught chest and a silver buckle belt helped keep his lusts under control. Isaac possessed none of these qualities, if qualities they could be called.

Life became very tough for Isaac after he split with Alice as her father had asked him to leave the company. He also had to leave the little house that he'd shared with Alice. Her father had given the house to her. Through no fault of his own, he had lost his wife, his job and his home. He also had to leave his faithful hound, Steam behind.

He wasn't bitter, just sad and down-trodden. He had known this wonderful woman for over eighteen years. They had loved each other, but the war does terrible things to people. Whilst Isaac fought for his country aboard the HMS Valour in the Battle of The Atlantic, Alice stayed at home with her mother and tried her best to live through the nightmare of Britain at war.

The sea beckoned. It had been in his blood all his life and he had read about a vacancy at a lighthouse on the east coast of Yorkshire. The chance to be the new lighthouse keeper suited his newfound lifestyle. He felt that he could be near the sea again and felt drawn to coast. His time in the navy gave him a lot of pride and he wanted to feel that again. Saving passing ships and boats from the cruel North Seas' anger would give him the chance to feel fulfilled again. He took what little money he had along with his few possessions with him. Upon arriving in Bridlington, he met with a representative from Trinity House who were and still are, responsible for all of the lighthouses around the coast of the United Kingdom. He would have a place to live and have food and supplies delivered to him regularly and would be able to smell the sea air every day. It sounded like the life he needed.

He received a letter from Alice that she had moved her lover into the house he had shared with her. Was she trying to hurt him? It seemed a rather cruel thing to do, he thought. Jake was a musician and played the guitar in a local group. Rock 'n roll was the sound of the fifties and Alice loved it and him. Alice explained that she felt as though she owed him an explanation but all it succeeded in doing was to upset him even more.

He settled into his life at the lighthouse well, and found that it was the thing which he had been missing all of his life. The views and the sea air began to reinvigorate him. The solitude was not an issue for him as he could indulge in his love of painting and fishing. He found a good friend in Peter Ambrose who began to visit regularly with provisions for Isaac and the lighthouse.

A year after he had moved to the coast, another letter arrived from his estranged wife. He knew the contents within without wondering what they would impart. She wanted a divorce so she could marry her rock 'n roller. He wasn't too surprised only that it had taken her so long to finally rip away the remains of his heart. He felt like an old fool now. He knew it had been over for twelve months, but his heart hurt reading the letter. He hadn't been much of a drinker in the past because he had a wife to look after and a job to keep. Now he just had his job and he was alone most days save for a visit from Peter who would bring his supplies every two weeks throughout the summer months. He had reached for the whiskey on the night of receiving the solicitor's letter. His head ached in the morning, but he felt better as he knew he needn't worry about his wife anymore. He loved her so much but knew that they should not have married. They had only met a few months before the beginning of the war and he had wanted something special to come home to. She had come into his life at the right time. A time where he needed the strength to get through the sheer nightmare that would become the Second World War.

The summer months of 1970 brought a more settled time to Isaac. The weather was warm in June but July failed to match up. The early part of the month saw record temperatures of ninety degrees Fahrenheit. Blue skies and beating hot Sun lasted just the one day and then the thunderstorms hit the very next day. So violent were these storms that no vessels dared venture out on the rough North Sea. The rest of the month remained cool and towards the south of the country ground frost formed at the shock of those living in Kent and Essex. At the end of the month heavy rain came down from the north and before summer really had a chance to shine it was over.

It was late September and Peter had just dropped off his bi-weekly supplies. There was no mention of the events which had happened earlier in the year as there was little point going over their fears and worries again. Let the wounds heal, they both thought. There had been no repeat of the dark shadow in the lantern room and Isaac had not experienced any bad dreams again. Although the thought of his Great Grandfather was still to the fore of his mind, he knew that there was nothing he could do to change things. They had happened one hundred years ago and that was that. He had to live his life and work hard to ensure no lives were lost due to his error.

Isaac was busy packing away the new intake as music filtered through the lighthouse. Whilst he went about his daily chores, Norman Greenbaum was raising his hands high in praise to the great "Spirit In The Sky". Isaac tuned in to Radio 4 to hear the weather forecast. The familiar voice stated "And now for the shipping forecast," followed by the news for all areas. He was listening out for Tyne and Dogger; his areas.

The forecaster obliged with "Tyne, Dogger, North East 4 or 5, rain then squally showers, poor becoming moderate."

It was almost six in the evening. Isaac checked the fog horn and removed a seagull which had become lodged inside. He retrieved the dead bird and placed it in a bag and secured it tightly. He then placed the bag and its content into the waste bin kept inside the fog horn hut. Peter would collect the refuse on his next visit and dispose of it safely back on land. A quick blast of the horns proved they were in good working order. As he ate his evening meal, the news told him of the death of a young guitarist, Jimi Hendrix. His mind went back eight years when he had found out about the death of his own wife and the man who she had loved more than him. Jake had the decency to take his own life although it was a cowardly move, in Isaac's mind. He felt no satisfaction at his death only the absolute devastation to find that Alice had been killed. It had been a most violent death at the hands of her lover at that. The accident was his fault and Isaac felt like he could have killed Jake himself. He was beginning to get agitated now. He recognised this and got to his feet and went to wash the dishes.

By ten that night, the rain had become to worsen and the horns were doing their job along with the beam of the light sweeping above. The waves started to increase in size and batter the rocks below. Isaac had gone through all the checks necessary and knew that he the lighthouse was secure and up to the task ahead. He stood in his bedroom watching the storm come in. He glanced across at the photographs displayed on his chest of drawers and focused on his wedding photo. He walked over and picked it up. When he had looked at this photo before, he had noticed that Alice wasn't looking at the camera. Now, her head had moved and was staring straight as Isaac. Wind whistled around the lighthouse with a steady rhythm. As Isaac studied the image Alice's eyes blinked. Without warning, the outer door to the lighthouse flew open bringing salty spray into Isaac's home. He heard the noise downstairs and dropped the photo to the floor and moved as quickly as he could manage. The frame gave way and the glass cracked.

As he reached the bottom floor the door rocked on its hinges while the driving rain washed his floor. Grabbing the handle, he tried to push the door closed, though he was met with some resistance. The wind and rain were strong but not that strong. The overhead light swung ferociously in the gale coming through the door. As he pushed again, the water brought seaweed in through the door which seemed to slither and worm its way in. Isaac watched the thing move slowly across the floor. Finally, he managed to close and lock the door again. He turned to face the mass of seaweed on the floor. Water shrank away from it as he watched it begin to shrivel in the warmth of the room. He could hear a faint crackle from the dying algae. A foul, stale, fishy smell emanated from the thing on the floor and he knew he had to get rid of it quickly before the stench made him sick. He had a large broom stored in the pantry and went to fetch it. As he passed the green slimy thing, it slowly moved towards his feet. He stared motionless. It moved again. The light overhead swung to a rest.

"That's all it was, the light," he said aloud.

He fetched the broom and began to sweep it into a green unctuous heap. The black bag he had taken from the cupboard was tucked into his belt. He withdrew it and speedily swept the thing into the bag's dark interior. Tying the bag tightly he dropped it into the large metal bin by the door. He'd take it out later and put it in the bin in the fog horn hut along with the deceased bird. Water drenched the floor so he mopped it up as best he could. Once the mess was cleaned up, his attention turned to the question of why the door had blown open at all. It had been securely locked as always and the bolts top and bottom had been shoved into place. Isaac had a very uneasy feeling about this. He studied the door for any signs that it had been tampered with or whether there was anything strange about it. Nothing seemed to be out of place. The bolts were damp from where he had pushed them into position and then he had locked the door. He had retrieved the key from its hook and locked the door. The key had been hanging on its usual hook yet the door had been opened by the storm. That was not supposed to happen. The door was made to withstand any force. He stood back to get a full view of the door. He traced its edges from top right down to the bottom, up the left hand side then across the top. Nothing was wrong with the door. He needed to check outside. The large flashlight stood in waiting next to the door. Wrapping his coat around him he unlocked then unbolted the door. He expected the door to fly open, thrust by an unseen phantom, but the door stayed shut. He took two deep breaths, picked up the torch and opened the door.

The wind whipped around his legs and the rain bit his face. He held on tightly to the rail and closed the door. The flashlight scanned the outer skin of the door. Two huge black marks stained the door at head height. Isaac brought the light close to the door to take a closer look. The white light of the torch touched the first blemish. He could make out green algae in the shape of a giant hand. He flinched at his discovery and looked across to the other mark. Some giant had pushed the door wide open. But it was locked and bolted, hadn't it? Isaac's brain raced to try and remember what had just happened. The seaweed had made him feel ill, but he was used to the smell and the sights that the sea had to offer. What was going on? The only explanation was that it had been opened from the inside. He was the only one in the lighthouse, wasn't he? His head started to ache as the news of this detection slowly crept into his brain. Someone was in the lighthouse with him. But who and where? How did they get in and when? Why did his dead wife's eyes blink at him from the photograph? He felt himself loose his balance and he dropped the flashlight to hold onto the rail with both hands. The torch rolled and lit up the path which led around to the fog horn and the boathouse. He followed is ghostly glare as its arc danced over the rocks and path and gasped at the sight which met his eyes. Broken wood covered the rocks and three bodies bobbed about in the clutter. He closed his eyes and heard a scream ricochet around his skull. No, not that, his mind said. It can't be them. Panic filtered from his brain to his body and he began to shake. He gripped the rail harder and tried to calm himself down. He put his head on the door and looked down at his feet. I'm dreaming, he thought. Not this time, his mind said. Look...

He looked straight up at the lighthouse and saw the light swing around regularly. Vertigo started to take over his mind and he closed his eyes and took a deep breath. When he opened them he counted the number of times that the light passed by over head. One, two, three then the final one stopped and shone its light out to sea. But what did it see? What did the light know? He watched it repeat this cycle twice before he took a breath and steadied himself. The shaking had stopped and he felt stronger now. Nothing was going to beat him. No threat, no-one, nothing. He felt the adrenalin flow through his body and he turned to face the horror on the rocks. He bent down to retrieve the torch and brought it around to the door. He let go of the rail and used his right sleeve to wipe away the ugly green marks.

Satisfied that they had gone, he turned his attention to the rocks. Wave after wave crashed into the debris and mixed the grotesque bodies in with the black wood. His breathing quickened as he moved around the lighthouse tower to look through the flotsam and jetsam. He could smell fumes and saw an oil patch sway in time with the waves. The smell and the swirling somehow got fiercer the closer he got. The flashlight moved over the chaos and he could pick out the black deformed bodies floating in the water. Rain drops sparkled in the ray of the flashlight. The bodies looked very much like the thing which had struck him those months ago. The one he had moved to the boathouse and carefully stashed in his boat; the one that had disappeared. Dead fish surrounded the rocks as well. Salmon, skate, scat. They looked to have been dead a while and the smell which accompanied their arrival kept the seagulls away. Isaac wanted to move them but his stomach couldn't handle the pungent reek. That and the burnt bodies created an atmosphere he didn't want to ever experience again.

Think, Isaac said to himself. Think. As he turned right to go and fetch the boat hook, his path was blocked by a tall grinning figure. All he could see were the teeth in the burnt head. It stood straight and tall and swayed gently from side to side unburdened by the wind and rain that threatened to take Isaac off his feet. Isaac staggered back and brought the light upon the horrific apparition before him. Black scales covered it from head to toe, skin burnt black to a crisp. Seaweed draped over its shoulders like a grim shawl. It stood still in the moonlight dripping with the seawater. Isaac could see that it had its eyes open wide but no eyes were visible in its sockets. It tilted its head back then lurched forward at him with a roar, bearing its white teeth as it came. It tried to grab at Isaac's coat but its talon-like fingers missed by an inch as Isaac jumped back and out of the way. Isaac stood his ground and swung the torch round and caught it on the jaw. The chin and lower jaw of the monster splintered off and flew into the waves. It turned again with foam spouting out of its wounded mouth. Isaac readied himself to strike again but as he did the thing stepped back. Its arms, legs and whole body disintegrated before him as an unholy howl came from its lipless mouth. The wind blew the black burnt ash into the sea and it was gone. Just a faint dark out-line remained. He turned to see the other bodies behind him. They too now turned to ash and swirled away into the wind and rain. Nothing remained. Even the fish and wood had disappeared. Only a faint aroma of death and decay mixed with the wind.

The storm died down and light rain patted onto the path. The sea calmed and the tiny splashes from the rain sounded like chips gently frying in a pan. He looked up and the moon had cleared the clouds completely now. Confusion and nausea took over his body. His legs buckled beneath him and he just managed to put his arms out to stop him going headfirst into the rocks below. He vomited over the path and wiped the sputum from his lips. His head pounded and he could hear his blood pulsing through his veins. What had just happened? I've got to get inside, he thought to himself. He struggled to his feet and wrapped his arm around the railing. He swung the torch back around to the left where the wood and bodies had been. The sea lapped gently against the rocks. He checked the torch and could see no sign of blood or gore there. He had hit that thing so hard there must be some evidence of it. The door! He remembered that he had wiped it clean. There was nothing to prove what he had seen. What about the seaweed and the water that came through the door? He hurried around to the door and walked inside. He opened the bin standing next to the door and looked inside. Paper, bent tins and a squashed box were the only contents. He slammed the door shut in anger. The awful taste of bile was still present in his mouth so he went through to the kitchen. Taking of his coat on the way, he hurled it across the back of his favourite chair and went to turn on the cold tap. He bent down and took a mouthful, swilled it around his mouth and spat it back into the sink. He filled a glass and went to sit down in his chair. Exhaustion took over his body and he fell unconscious.

Daylight came through the tiny window in the lighthouse living quarters. A glass lay broken on the floor at the feet of the sleeping Isaac Shepherd. Outside, the seabirds were making their usual noise. Feeding, flying and fighting. He opened his eyes and looked around his home. His hand went up to his forehead and rubbed, trying to rid himself of his terrible headache. He sat up and stretched his stiff neck. He rolled his shoulders up to his ears and brought his arms up over his head and stretched the out until he heard a loud crack.

"Still alive then?" he said aloud. Was he disappointed in the fact, he thought grimly. He was still wearing his heavy boots and thick jumper. He rubbed his neck and stood up. His left leg didn't want to play this morning, and his knee gave way. He slumped back into the chair.

"Too quick," he said.

What had happened last night? What the hell was going on?

He needed to get washed. He looked at the door and noticed that he hadn't locked or bolted it. If there was something out there wanting to get in after he collapsed, nothing would have stopped it. No bolt, no lock. He tried to stand again and this time he managed it. He walked over to the door and opened it wide. The only thing that came in was the fresh salty taste of the sea. Three deep breathes later and he felt a little more human. He managed to climb the steps up to his bedroom and saw the broken glass in the frame on the floor. He reached down to pick it up and a wave of nausea hit him again. He staggered and put his hand to his forehead. He sat down gently on the floor and picked up the picture frame. He turned it over in his hands and studied the photograph. The glass had broken so he took the old photograph out of its frame and brought it close to his eyes. The picture was as it had always been. Neither Isaac nor Alice looked happy in the image. Still holding the photo he bent his head down and cried.

The sea was calm and the sky had painted wisps of white cloud. The nightmare of what had happened or not last night, seemed to have happened to someone else. In another place somewhere far away from this idyllic place. Isaac washed and dressed then made himself a mug of black coffee. He stepped out onto the path and walked around the lighthouse. The rocks gleamed in the sunshine as tiny waves played upon the surface of the sea. Isaac walked around the whole lighthouse tower watching the birds fly overhead. His head still ached and the vision of the dark beast he had seen last night was etched like cruel words on the gravestone of his memory. His stomach turned at the thought of it and he started to worry about his sanity. He needed to know why these things were happening to him.

He stepped back though the door and threw the bolts and locked the door. He stared at the large white heavy door and wondered how it could have been forced open like it had been last night. The simple answer was that it couldn't have. It was made to withstand the most violent of storms. He had to think logically about this. He took out a notepad and a pen and sat down in his chair. He made some notes:

1) *The door was locked from the inside and the key was on its hook*

2) *Both the top and bottom bolts were secured*

3) *There is no sign of the seaweed*

4) *There is no sign of the wood or bodies*

5) *You're going crazy*

He looked at what he had written. Yes, he thought, that just about covers it. It cannot have happened the way he thought it had. He had so many thoughts going through his head at the moment that his brain had somehow misfired and made something into a reality that wasn't real. His visit to York, finding out about his Great Grandfather, the disturbing dream he'd had about Peter's death. Crazy or not, the events he thought had happened last night couldn't have happened. He needed to eat.

After breakfast, he called the coast guard to find out how things had gone with them last night.

"Nothing to report really, Isaac," Tom had said.

There had been no incidents to speak of. A fishing trawler had broken down about eight miles off shore and the life boat had been dispatched. The new crew managed to tow the boat to safety with no real problem. He signed off and switched off the little Bush radio.

The chores lay ahead of him, but he couldn't muster up the energy to do anything. He decided to try and get some decent sleep and set off to his bed. He stopped and looked at the room around him. It was his home and he needed to defend it. He needed sleep, so sat in the chair and put the radio back on. Radio Four played its soothing classical music. The shipping forecast would be broadcast around midday and he wanted to hear it. He hoped he'd wake up when it was on. He took a couple of tablets with a glass of water and settled into his chair. He slept though he didn't dream.

He managed to wake up just before noon and he listened to the forecast. He felt a lot better. Things seemed to be going very strange for him lately. So many ups and downs and nothing constant. He thought about Pete's offer some months ago about staying with him and Sally. He thought that he needed a break from the lighthouse after all this time. He wouldn't be seeing Peter for another couple of weeks as he had just brought his delivery yesterday and he needed to check with Trinity House before he had a break anyway. He could call through to Tom, the coast guard and ask him to relay his message to Peter. They would need to get him some cover though. He couldn't see there being a problem as he'd not taken a holiday at all since arriving there more than twelve years previously. He could come over during the day and make sure everything was alright. He decided to write to them to officially ask for some time off then speak with Peter. He knew that Peter would have no problem with him staying with him and his wife. With renewed vigour he decided to listen to the weather forecast.

"And now for the shipping forecast." He learned that the weather should be better today and tonight with maybe a slight fog throughout the night. He switched it off. He went to his bathroom and readied himself for the rest of the day. A quick call was made through to Tom then Isaac started on his daily chores. He decided that a full clean of the inside of the lighthouse was called for today. He walked down to the kitchen to fetch the mop and bucket. As he picked up the mop he noticed it was wet. Wet from mopping the floor last night when the door blew in! His head felt light again as he steadied himself. He then looked in the pantry and saw that the small window had a crack in it. Rain or seawater had seeped through the crack and dripped into the bucket, soaking the mop. He gave a little nervous laugh and went to fetch some tape to temporarily mend the window.

Isaac washed down all the surfaces and mopped the floor. He opened the door and let the fresh sea breeze bring in the smells of the sea. The watch room needed a little tidying which took him no time at all. A distant worry still sat at the back of his mind. A little voice telling him not all was well. He tried to shrug away the feeling but it kept coming back. There was something that he hadn't checked. He went back to last night and knew that he hadn't been dreaming. The bodies and the wood had been there. The black figure he attacked was there. He could feel a twinge in his right shoulder where he had swung the flashlight at its head. But there was still a concern he had that he had left undone. He mentally went through his list again. His coat, he thought. "I rubbed the door clean with my coat sleeve."

He walked back down to the ground floor and saw his coat swinging gently in the sea breeze. Hesitating slightly, Isaac moved the coat sleeve into view. With trepidation, he checked the arm. A filthy green sludge stain covered the sleeve. This was the only evidence he had found from the previous night and it filled him with fear again. Buzzing sounds fizzed through his head. Panic! He had to do something. He put on his boots, threw the coat over his shoulders and walked out into the bright afternoon sunshine. He checked the door again, more closely this time and found a very faint green residue smeared into its surface. He steadily walked around the path to where he had seen the wood and the badly burnt bodies. He couldn't see anything. He went to get the boat hook just as he had planned last night before the monster appeared. Unlocking the hook with unsteady hands was difficult. After a moment, the key went into the lock and he retrieved the long pole. Moving back around to the rocks, he reached out with the hook and began slowly dredging the water. He made large sweeping motions as the pole dipped into the water. He felt the pole hit something below the water and turned the pole to see if he could hook anything. Something caught hold and he tried to pull it onto the rocks. The sky darkened and a distant rumble advertised the coming of a storm. Isaac pulled at the pole and the netting rose to the surface. He dragged it over the rocks and climbed down to inspect his find. The fishing net had caught something and held its haul tightly. Isaac pulled out his knife and began to cut into the net. He split the net open to reveal burnt wood. The netting must have come loose from one of the fishing boats, maybe the one which had broken down out there last night. The wood was black and had turned into charcoal. He fished around the nets innards and found more wood until he touched something different. Revulsion made with move his hand away quickly. It was a body. He could see a charred arm sticking out of the wood. His heart thumped heavily in his chest as another rumble in the sky broke the silence. He had to bring the whole net up out of the water. He got hold of the hook and reached further into the water to try and hoist the ghastly coffin out. He couldn't move it. The net was either too heavy or stuck on some unseen snag. He decided to get a hold of the net with the hook and try to fasten the other end to the railing. He managed to attach the hooks and making sure that they were secure, walked back around the lighthouse and through its door. He called the coast guard and told Tom what he had found. Tom told him to wait outside with the net and the life boat would come around and try and release the net and its dead cargo.

Isaac felt as though the nightmares and the strange things which had been happening were due to the awful object which had attached itself to the rocks of the lighthouse. Ghosts of the dead seamen were haunting the lighthouse and getting through and into his brain. Would that all go once the dead had been removed?

As he waited outside, he saw the thunderheads gather on the horizon and a flash split sky in two. Its black clouds seemed to get darker after the flash. The rumble followed a few moments later. He could see the haze of driving rain obscure the horizon now as another lightning bolt lit up the clouds. The familiar sound of the life boat came around the coast line to the south and Isaac waved to it. A blast from its horn signalled its arrival and he smiled to himself. Please hurray, he thought to himself. He wanted rid of the net and its hoard.

The boat came along side the lighthouse as its new captain, Alex Freeman called across to him.

"Isaac, sounds like you've found something nasty. You okay?"

"Better for seeing you, Alex. Can you get to the net?" Isaac shouted back.

Alex called back to his crew as the boat dipped and rocked on the waves. The boat came a little closer now. Isaac unhooked the pole and walked around and onto the rocks near the life boat. Another flash was followed quickly by another clap of thunder. He managed to pass the hook up to Alex. Two crew members appeared with long hooks themselves and caught hold of the net. As they steadied the grotesque rigging and its catch, a third crew member moved the winch over to the stricken net and with help of Isaac and the others, tightly secured the net. After a moment or two, the net came free and it sailed into the air swaying in the wind which had started to come in from the storm. Black water seeped out of the net and back into the ocean below. It was gently levered around then lowered onto the deck of the boat. The net sagged and opened up when it touched the deck. Alex moved over to check its contents and found wood, fish a few crabs and three badly scorched dead bodies.

"We've found three bodies here, Isaac," shouted Alex over the sound of the wind.

Isaac was rooted to the spot and felt both relief and upset to hear his message.

"Three?" he questioned.

"It looks like it."

If these were three of the members of the life boat which exploded in the water some months ago, then one body was yet to be found. There was still the sixth. No doubt it was the fiend that had stood on this very path last night showing its sharp white angry teeth at him. A chill ran through him. It's still out there, a voice spoke to him inside.

"We'll get these ashore and pass them over to the authorities," Alex yelled back.

The wind had picked up even more now.

Isaac motioned back to him and waved.

With the netting and its horrific contents now safely on their way back to shore, Isaac retreated into his home. He closed the door and stood there, staring into nothing. His mind raced, trying to understand what this meant.

"It means that three families can finally have some closure on this tragedy and can now grieve," he said aloud. The last twenty four hours had taken its toll on him, but he knew he had a duty to do. He busied himself with his jobs and put the radio back on. "Hancock's Half Hour" was on. Anthony was a famous pilot and could hear knocking as he flew thousands of feet in the sky.

"Oh, hello," said Kenneth Williams.

The moonlight crept across the floor of the bedroom and found the three paintings hanging above his father's chest of drawers. Isaac's seascapes each featured ships and small boats fighting the high winds of the North Sea. In the months and years since he had added paint to canvas, the ships and sea had remained inert; silent. Tonight, as the silver light of the moon shone over the paintings, waves swept up and over the frames. Isaac awoke with a start at the noise. It sounded as though the sea had come through the window and was threatening to drown him.

The large sails of the huge sailing ship flapped noisily as the wild winds took the ship from the left painting across the confines of the wooden picture frame and into the path of the flotilla of boats struggling with the storm in the centre painting. The hulls of the wooden ships creaked and cursed as they fought to stay afloat. More water foamed out of the painting and onto the wooden surface of the chest and drenched the pictures below. The sailing ship crashed on through the waves toward the small fleet and threatened to destroy them with its sheer weight and aggression. It smashed into the sea and created a massive wave which covered four of the small boats. Broken wood splinters rained down on the old piece of furniture below.

Isaac sat up in his bed watching the scene play out before his eyes. His dry mouth hung loose as he watched his paintings come to life. He felt a panic freeze his bones. Lightning flashed across all three paintings and lit up the room with its white blinding light. His eyes stung with the sudden white blast. He blinked a few times and rubbed at his sore eyes. When his eyesight re-aligned itself in the dark he looked up at the paintings and they were as they had always been. He gingerly stepped out of his bed and cautiously walked over to study his paintings. He slowly put his hands towards the middle painting and stretched out his fingers. The familiar bumps and peaks of the rough paint met his fingers as he slowly caressed the canvas.

He placed his hands onto the top of the chest of drawers and leaned in close to get a better look. Nothing had changed in any of his paintings. Suddenly, a sharp pain shot through his left hand and he winced, drawing in a quick gasp. The top and side of the chest of drawers were wet and covered in foul dank seaweed. He stepped back holding his hand and walked over to his bed. He switched on the bedside light and opened his hand. A splinter of wood stuck out of his palm and a red stream had started to flow out of the wound. He carefully pinched the wood between his thumb and forefinger and pulled the short sword out of his skin. As he pulled, his skin ripped open and Isaac could see four small twisted pins attached to the end of the splinter. He brought it up to the light and stared at it. It resembled a short pole with four hooks attached. A grappling hook!

He gently placed it on the window sill and walked through to his bathroom. His hand had begun to throb as he washed away the dark thick blood. He dabbed at the wound and saw a small cross at the centre of his palm. Four triangular flaps of skin revealed a dark red hole at the centre. The stinging had begun to subside. He pressed his thumb into the wound and a thick blue viscous liquid spread over his hand. He thrust it back into the sink and turned on the tap again. The torn skin eased and the rich blue liquid thinned and stopped. It had a faint smell of ammonia and Isaac's head began to feel heavy. He staggered backwards and hit the door behind him. His legs gave way and he fell to the floor with a heavy thud. His right elbow connected with the wall and his head twisted and cracked on the floor. His vision faded and he blacked out.

The morning sunlight replaced the moon's glow and Isaac opened his eyes. He lay in bed. He ran his left hand through his hair and slowly sat up. His neck felt stiff and his head buzzed. He couldn't remember getting back into his bed. The previous night's event came back to his brain. He looked down at his left palm and saw no sign of the vicious wound. The paintings opposite his bed looked the same as they did when he had painted them. The seaweed which had been draped over the chest of drawers had gone as had the smell. He stepped out of bed and walked over the chest of drawers as he had done in the middle of the night. He looked at the pictures and the furniture. Same as they ever were.

The hook, he thought; the window sill. He rushed over to where he had placed the tiny grappling hook but no sign of it remained. He looked down to see if it had fallen off onto the floor below: nothing. As he knelt there he began to cry. What was happening to him? It didn't feel like a dream but then again it couldn't have been real. No wound, no small hook, no water. He put his hands to his face as he sobbed. His salty tears covered both of his hands as he rubbed them into his eye sockets. A sharp pain shot through his left hand and he drew it away from his face and stared at it. A faint white cross appeared in the centre of his hand. It looked like a very old scar which had healed over time. The pain stopped as soon as it had started. He scratched at the cross with his nails trying to open the flesh. He stopped and looked again. Red scratch marks covered his hand but the white cross remained.

CHAPTER SEVEN

A long distant sound

Around ears that don't hear

There must me some life

A long way from here

He had loved Alice in spite of everything that had happened, but he also knew that there was no point in fighting it. He had signed the solicitor's letter and sent it back to the address typed at the bottom of the embossed letter. Within a few months his married had been declared null and void. Alice sent a letter to him yet another asking for forgiveness. She said that while she had loved him before the war, her life had been put on hold whilst he was away fighting and she could not be sure that he would ever return.. She knew that she should have waited for him but that life was not that simple. Isaac didn't reply. He tore the letter in two and watched it take to the wind like one of the seagulls. The two white halves drifted off in different directions much like Alice and Isaac had.

Her new husband enjoyed some minor success playing at local parties and concert halls. A record deal was offered to his group which they duly signed and were promised the full backing of the record company and were paid an advance. They made a record which received plenty of airplay and their shows drew large crowds of young ladies wanting to share a glimpse of their new rock 'n roll heroes.

Jake's love of fast cars had led him to import a Cadillac Eldorado Biarritz from the States. Its large fins and chromed good looks made a real statement in England. It was brash and loud, just like the music he played. He would take Alice out into the country for drives and show how well he could handle this monster of a car. They used to drive and Alice would laugh whilst the wind blew her hair around her face.

On the fateful day of her death, Alice laughed and sang at the top of her voice to Jake's new hit record. She held onto the front windscreen's frame with one hand and clicked the fingers of the other in time to the music. As the car came over the brow of a hill Alice screamed with joy. Jake hadn't seen the tractor parked at the side of the road over the blind summit. The car's wheels left the road momentarily and as the contact with road resumed, Jake lost control of the powerful car and hit the large mechanical beast head on. The convertible car held little protection for neither driver nor passenger. Alice had been standing up as the car reached the top of the small rise in the road and had been holding onto the windscreens frame with just her left hand. The force of the impact propelled her straight over the windscreen of the car and through the windscreen of the tractor. Her head collided so violently that her skull had been pushed into her body; she died instantly. Jake was thrown at the windshield, but his seat belt held fast and through him back into his seat. The air was taken from him and he sat there dazed and confused. Jake broke his left arm and collar bone in the accident but his heart never stood a chance. Like Isaac before him, Jake heart broke into shattered pieces at the loss of Alice. The driver of the tractor had seen the car fly over the rise in the road and had managed to prepare himself for the impact. He had jumped down from his cab and torn three ligaments in his left ankle in the process. He would need to wear a cast on his leg for four of five weeks but would otherwise be unscathed. Jake unfastened the seat belt and crawled out of the wreckage to try and find Alice. Her body had been broken and mangled as her legs lay lifelessly on top of the tractors engine whilst the top half of her body mingled in with the smashed windscreen and twisted metal of the tractors cab. Metal and flesh converged and it was difficult to see where Alice finished and the vehicle started. Jake wept and wailed at the sight of the love of his life. Great sobs jolted his entire body as he shook from head to toe. Her shoes lay discarded on the road as he picked them up and cradled then close to his chest. He rocked back and forth, his tears streaking his face. The driver of the tractor managed to make his way over to Jake and asked him if he was alright. Jake just sat there, rocking. He sat like that until the police arrived and lead him to their patrol car. As he sat in the back of the patrol car, his face was set in a mask of horror. His once pretty-boy looks where scarred and broken. The ambulance medics checked Jake then went to see to what could be done for Alice. They managed to extract her from the wreckage and took her to the nearest hospital. Her body was taken to the ambulance and loaded inside on the bed on the left. Jake was cleaned up and after a preliminary check was also placed in the ambulance. The lay him down on the opposite bed to Alice and secured him there for the short journey to the hospital. Alice's body was covered in a cotton sheet as red blood patches stained the pristine shroud. Jake managed to move his head over to stare at her form as dirty tears dried on his face. His eyes didn't leave her throughout the trip. Upon arriving at the hospital, Alice's body was taken away and Jake was patched up and sent on his way. The police detained him at the local station for what seemed like a life-time, then the police charged him with dangerous driving and allowed him to go.

Jake couldn't live without his beloved wife and two nights after the devastating crash he sat at their home after being released by the police. He held his head in his hands and sobbed. The wealth from his success meant nothing to him now. He just wanted Alice back in his life. He wanted to see her again. He undid his belt and looped it around the light cord in their bedroom. He then fastened the other end around his neck and kicked away the chair.

Isaac had avoided listening to Radio One in the past for fear of ever hearing one of those songs his late ex-wife's second husband had recorded. He had learned about their untimely deaths and hated Jake even more than he dared think possible. Her life had been taken in such a violent way. Jake had lived with the loss of Alice for a very short time in a tormented living hell. Had he killed himself rather than face his life without Alice or was it that he couldn't deal with the press headlines saying that he had killed his wife? Isaac didn't know or care about Jake. Alice was dead. Isaac had attended Alice's funeral although he had not wanted to be seen, so stood some distance from the small crowd. The small circle of trees would hide him from their sight. As he scanned their faces he noticed that her mother and father were there. Alice's mother was in a wheelchair and didn't look as if she knew exactly what was happening. Her father had his left hand on her shoulder all the way through the service as he stood by the graveside. Of the other mourners he only recognised two of her friends, Anne and Maggie. Both looked so much older than he remembered them and if they saw him he was sure that they'd say the same thing about him. A number of people, acquaintances, friends or work colleagues surrounded the dirt hole in the ground. Two people did stand out though. A young couple, maybe eighteen or nineteen huddled close to each other. After the coffin was lowered, the small crowd began to disperse. Only her parents and the young couple remained. The grave digger stood patiently behind them and, as soon as left he began his morbid duty. Isaac watched from afar. Once the grave digger had completed his task and had walked away for a well deserved cup of sweet tea and his sandwiches, he walked over to the grave and placed a single white rose on the newly laid soil. "Goodbye darling," he said. He hadn't seen her for so long and found it difficult to come to terms that he'd never see her again. The only picture he had of her was of their wedding day. He struggled with his emotions and tears glazed his eyes. He sniffed and wiped them away. As he left the cemetery, he turned and saw that the teenage boy was watching him from the black funeral car.

Six days after his horrible find, he received a call from Tom.

"Isaac, the bodies have been examined, and it looks as though they are three of the missing crew. Dental records have shown that you found Robert, Andrew and Warren. We've yet to find George. It was a miracle that the net caught a hold of those three."

"Yes, a miracle indeed." Isaac knew that George wouldn't be found. He had moved on to a different plane of existence.

"Please pass my condolences and sorrow onto the families, would you? And Peter, does he know?"

"Thanks, Isaac. I will. Yes, Peter was told when the bodies had been brought back to the harbour."

"How did he take it?"

"About as well as can be expected I suppose."

Isaac switched off the radio and sat back in his chair looked up at the ceiling. Five of the bodies had been found and yet George Meade was still unaccounted for. Isaac walked over to the bathroom and placed his hands on the sink and looked at his reflection in the mirror. He rubbed his chin and moved closer to the mirror image. He looked older than his fifty three years. These last few months had aged him greatly.

He took of his jumper and his vest and turned to check his shoulder. The bruise was almost gone now but the dull pain still remained. He dressed and wandered through the lighthouse aimlessly. His mind raced and wondered whether he may get another visit from George's ghost.

It was mid-October when it was announced that British Petroleum, the global oil company had found a huge oil field one hundred and ten miles east of Aberdeen in the North Sea. More ships were going to be heading out through the North Sea and the lighthouse was kept busy. Constant chatter filled the airwaves as many vessels travelled in these waters. For Isaac, life seemed to be normal. Rain and fog were the main issues and the fog horn had a busier time than Isaac. It had been working perfectly well for the last couple of years, but on the night of October 31st, it decided to break down altogether.

He had run the routine test earlier in the day and it was working absolutely normally. There were no issues. The horns were clear and the power was fine. However, when the fog hit the bay at eight thirty, the horns fell silent. The horn had broken back in 1967 and Isaac had managed to mend it then and was sure he'd be able to fix it now. The toolbox held everything he should need and he got himself ready. His ear-defenders hung by the door. He put them on. Unlocking the door still felt strange to him after the discovery of the life boat crew washed up in the netting stuck to the rocks. Each time he opened it, he felt the dread shoot through his body.

Peter had been to see him after his find. He said that it wouldn't really be possible for Isaac to stay with Sally and himself at the moment. They had been to the service of three of his friends again as the bodies were buried alongside their two colleagues. Sally had got very upset again as had Peter. He'd been strong for her, but he was having a hard time as well. The overriding sorrow was highlighted by the fact that one body was still missing. The fright that Peter had experienced at the lighthouse was still in the back of his mind. He felt less comfortable there but wanted to help his dear old friend as best he could.

The heavy fog shrouded the lighthouse as Isaac stepped out onto the path. He leant against the door as it clicked shut. The light above was doing its best to break through the veil of fog, but he didn't think that it was making much of an impression. He passed the boathouse and unlocked the door to the fog horn house. He flicked the light switch but nothing happened. He didn't expect anything else. He moved the flash light around the interior and moved through to the fuse box. Shining the light into the box, he could see that two of the fuses had blown and tripped the whole system. The tool box contained the relevant fuses and within a few moments the power had been restored. The room lit up and the generator belched into life. He checked the cramped room to make sure that everything was in order. It was. He turned and left just as the deafening blast rumbled through the dense fog. Even though his ears were protected the deep thrum of the horn rattled his bones. He once more stepped out onto the path to make his way back indoors. The fog was the thickest he could remember ever seeing in his time on these rocks. It was so thick that it had no movement to it. It just hung there motionless in the night. The light of the lighthouse was doing its job as it swung around three times, then stopped. Its bright light cut through the fog to give succour to any vessel that dared trespass into the grey domain beyond.

The door to the lighthouse was wide open when he returned. Isaac put down the tool box and opened it. The heavy hammer felt good in his right hand. This is it, he thought to himself, could this be the time to meet and great my maker? His heart beat harder in his chest and threatened to burst out and split his ribcage. In his left hand, the trusty flash light was turned off. His thumb hovered over the button ready to illuminate whatever had gone inside. He mustered all of his energy and ran in through the door, screaming and waving the lethal hammer through the air ready to connect with whoever or whatever it was that waiting for him inside his own home. A seaweed and water trial weaved its way through the door and over to the kitchen area. The lights were off in the room so he flicked the small switch on the torch and followed the damp pathway. The light shone through the darkness onto the moist floor. Its beam picked up the trial and as he moved it forward and upward discovered what had made the mess. A man lay in a heap on the floor. It looked like a man, but it was difficult to ascertain. It looked more like a jumble sale of old coats than of anything living. He stepped forward still gripping the hammer. The thing on the floor didn't move. As he got closer he could see that it was an old man with long matted grey hair. His matching beard was covered in dank seaweed and salt water. Isaac moved him with his foot and the figure slumped over onto its back. Black cancerous sores covered most of his face. Isaac felt the urge to finish him off now with the hammer and put him out of his misery. He could see the man's chest slowly rise and fall. He was alive. He turned on the lights and flicked off the flash light. The man weighed a tonne as he tried to lift him up. The dead weight proved difficult for him but after a few minutes he had managed to get him into his chair. The man's clothes were ripped and torn. His boots had no laces. The trousers were tatters and he could see the man was wearing stained long-johns underneath. The coats were the strange thing though. As Isaac peeled them back he counted five layers of coats. Under those he wore a shirt with no collar. Isaac didn't want to get too close as the stench which partnered his new guest was the worst he had ever smelled. He could hear very shallow breaths coming from the man's raw lips. He left him in the chair and went to fetch some water for him. He had no idea who he was or how he had got here but

Isaac had to do something for him. His initial plan to kill the thing which had made its way into his home had now gone. He lifted the man's head and wet his lips. A rancid tongue flicked out to get to the water. The mouth opened slightly and Isaac poured the liquid into it.

Concern and sympathy took over Isaac's thoughts as he lifted the man's head so he could get to the water easier. It was then when he opened his eyes. The man had dark brown eyes with tiny pupils. Isaac could see that the light was hurting his eyes so turned the chair around and away from the overhead light. The man opened his mouth as if to speak but no voice came out, just a quiet groan. When the man looked up at Isaac his eyes became wider and his mouth again opened as if to scream. He then went limp and his eyes and mouth clamped shut. Exhaustion had taken over and the man now lay unconscious once more.

Isaac had managed to loosen the coats and placed a warm blanket over the man. By the looks of him he must have been in his mid sixties although the terrible state he was in could have aged him greatly. Isaac took the coats over to the kitchen light and examined them one by one. The first was the one the man had been wearing over all of the others and was in a terrible state. He checked through the pockets but found nothing other than seaweed. He draped it over the chair behind him. The second one was in much the same shape as the first. It was as tattered as the other but there was something in the pockets. As he dug into the first one he was mindful of what he might find. He took out his hand and tipped the coat upside down and shook it aggressively. A knife and a small ball of string fell out of one. Three pebbles fell out of the other. The knife looked vicious and well used. The handle was well worn and the blade had small nicks out of it. He brushed them aside into a small pile.

The third coat was in a better condition than either of the first two and a much better coat all round. The embroidery was of a very fine standard and the lining, though ripped had the feel of an expensive silk. He turned it around to inspect it and found that something rattled in the pockets. Not wanting to risk a cut from a rusty blade he shook the contents out and onto the floor. A necklace of stunning quality snaked onto the damp floor and a tiny ring came to rest by it. He bent down and wrapped his fingers around the necklace and brought it up to the light for a better view. The stones gleamed in the overhead lamp and a beautiful prism displayed delicate white, blue and yellow light. He was no expert of such finery but those looked like diamonds and sapphires to him. The gold ring too shone in the darkness. It matched the ring with stunning precious jewels. It had three of the deepest blue sapphires he had ever seen. A solitary diamond nestled between the three blue stones. He carefully placed the jewellery onto the draining board beside the sink.

The fourth coat was a suit jacket of the sort Isaac had never seen. Gold brocade decorated the neck and front. A red and gold lining lay beneath the wonderful black jacket. The pockets gave up more treasures. Medals and coins lay heavy in the silk lined pockets. He tried to see the details on one of the medals but could only make out two letters: VR. "Victoria Regina," he said aloud turning to the old man sleeping in his chair. The coins were even more difficult to read than the medals but they too looked very old.

The fifth coat was actually a waistcoat. Isaac felt brave enough to feel in the pockets this time. Isaac gently pulled at the chain and a watch slipped out of the pocket. A silver pocket watch was still firmly attached to its chain. He held it to his ear and could hear a faint ticking noise coming from the case. He undid the clasp and opened the lid of the watch. The hands moved around with beautiful precision. The glass cover was intact and he could read the name "American Watch Co" written across the face. A small second hand movement had its own place at the bottom of the face. What struck him was that the minute hand on the watch was exactly correct although the hour hand was not. The watch felt to have a good balance in his hand as he placed it carefully by the sink along with the other items. The other pocket held a silver cigarette case with the initials "RK" inscribed. He turned it over in his hand admiring the quality. He pressed the release button on the side and it flipped open. Four saturated cigarettes lay inside. A striking block was positioned at the base for igniting the match to light the cigarette. This had been used extensively as it was blackened. He emptied the water into the sink and placed the damp white sticks in the bin under the basin.

He studied the items he had found. The necklace, ring, medals, coins, watch and case sat side by side on the draining board. The man behind him stirred and gave a grunt and turned his head to one side, yet remained fast asleep. Isaac paused until he saw that the man didn't move again then went back to look at the hoard. The items must be worth quite a pretty penny at any auction house and Isaac assumed that this ravaged old man had obviously stolen them from somewhere. The multitude of coats was strange though. Why not put everything into one pocket? He was no clearer as to where this strange person had come from. He gathered the contraband and carefully wrapped them in a towel he kept next to the sink. Steadily, he placed the towel underneath the sink and closed the cupboard door.

He checked his own watch again and it read fifteen minutes past ten. His uninvited guest lay still but every now and then would jolt in his sleep and his mouth would open and close. No real sound came forth just a quiet whine. Isaac needed to sleep but didn't want to leave this man here whilst he slept. Who knows what this man was capable of doing? He looked old and dishevelled and Isaac was sure that he was a good match for him if they got into a fight. But not if he slept, he thought. Isaac looked around the room and saw the rope curled in the corner. The long length of rope was used for throwing to Peter on those days when the sea was too rough to approach the lighthouse. Isaac would throw the rope to Peter who would in turn tie the provisions for Isaac to his end of the rope. Peter had plenty of water proof bags on board to keep any of Isaac's goods clean and dry. He had to tie this man up securely until morning. The chances were that Isaac would wake before him anyway. The man looked more than tired and he thought that he would be alright. No need to take any chances, he said to himself. He took the rope and began to tie the man's hands together then loop the rope under the chair and around his legs. He then brought the rope over the back of the chair and tied it around his chest. The rope was then tied with a half hitch. He stepped back to look at this man. Was it unfair to tie him up like this? He had to be careful as he had no knowledge of who this man was or how he got here. He'd sleep down here tonight. He went up to his own bed and brought down a thick blanket and wrapped it around himself. By midnight, they both slept.

Isaac opened his eyes and saw the man looking at him. Thankfully, he was still sat in the chair tied to it like a criminal. In Isaac's mind he was a criminal. He'd come into his home and had very expensive looking trinkets in his pockets. The man stared at Isaac with fear in his eyes. Isaac got up, stretched and looked into the man's face. The smell was still really bad, but Isaac spoke.

"Right, I'm going to untie you now and I don't want you to do anything stupid. Okay?" he said nodding at the man.

His blank eyes fixed Isaac's but he did not move.

"Do you understand me?" Isaac tried again.

The man slowly nodded and looked Isaac up and down.

"Alright." Isaac untied the man's bonds and began to store the rope.

The man rubbed his shoulders and tugged the blanket close around his body. He kept a fix on Isaac as he moved about the room.

"Food?" Isaac motioned using a knife and fork.

Again, the man nodded.

"Alright." Isaac stepped into the kitchen to start making some food for the both of them. The man stayed where he was, not wanting to move or flinch.

He put the food in front of his guest and he started to eat. The man looked down and picked up the fork. He took a piece of bacon and brought it to his nostrils and took a deep breath. He smiled and put it into his mouth and started to chew. For the first time, he took his eyes off Isaac although Isaac kept a careful watch on him. They both finished off the cooked breakfast and Isaac went to fetch a mug of tea for each of them. He offered the hot mug to the man and he looked up at Isaac. He took it and put it to his lips.

"It's hot, be careful," and Isaac blew across the surface of the tea. Small ripples rapidly crossed the black surface of the tea.

"Who are you?" Isaac came straight to the point.

The man sat and stared at him.

"Where are you from?"

Still, the man just sat there.

You're not going to make this easy, are you? he thought to himself.

"I'm Isaac," he said and held out his hand.

The man's reaction was violent and unexpected. He lurched for the door and Isaac managed to grab him and pushed him back into the chair.

"Hold on, there," Isaac shouted.

The man slumped back into the chair still very agitated.

"You're the one who came into my house, I'm the one who should be angry," Isaac fumed. Throw him out, he thought.

The man settled. He nodded slowly at Isaac.

"Right then. Who are you?"

The man opened his mouth trying to speak, but nothing happened. His red raw lips and tongue tried to say something. He held his throat and shook his head.

The man seemed to understand Isaac, but could not talk. His grey matted hair looked like a life form of its own and the sores on his face looked so severe that Isaac expected them to erupt and leave nothing but a skinned skull. The cream grey underclothes he was wearing didn't look as though they were doing anything to keep him warm. Isaac could see that what he really needed was a bath. He didn't like the thought of this thing bathing in his bathroom but he knew that he had to do something.

"I'll run you a bath," Isaac told the man, although it sounded more like a question to his ears.

The man nodded appreciatively.

Isaac eyed the cupboard under the sink where he had stashed the items this man had brought into the lighthouse. The coats he had been wearing were piled on the floor in the kitchen. He had to move them so that this dishevelled man wouldn't realise that he had taken his precious haul. He moved through the kitchen and kicked the clothes towards the bottom of the steps then bent down to pick them up. He tucked the coats under his left arm away from the prying eyes of the tramp like huddle sat in his chair clutching the tea mug closely to his chest. He stuffed the coats underneath his bed and went to run a bath. The steam soon fogged the window as the hot water splashed into his old bath. He fetched an old towel and set it down by the bath.

The man sat staring at him when he got back down stairs. He hadn't moved. That's good, thought Isaac; at least I seem to have the upper hand. He motioned to his shoulders that he was cold and seemed to be looking around the room for his coats.

"You can use my clothes," Isaac said. He reached his hand out to help him stand, but he shied away from Isaac's touch.

"Bath. You're bath is ready. I'll get you some clean clothes."

He looked up at him with baleful eyes as though Isaac had offered to throw him naked into the sea. Isaac was trying to help the man, why would he react like this? Isaac tried to coax him out of the chair and eventually he tried to stand. Isaac held onto him beneath his arms and immediately regretted it. It felt as though something was moving underneath his decrepit clothing. Isaac attempted to keep his composure but he found it very difficult. He was already regretting drawing a bath for this…man.

Throw him out, came the voice in his head.

He took small tentative steps and managed to get to the bottom of the stairs without falling. He looked up at the stairs winding up above him then looked at Isaac. It didn't look like he could manage climbing them, but still he tried. He got his right foot on the bottom step and Isaac gave him a little push. Each step seemed to take a lot of energy out of him although, after almost five minutes of climbing he reached the next floor. The bath sat below the window with a small chair positioned to the right of it. He stopped to rest and put his right hand on the back of the chair. There wasn't much room in the circular room. He looked around at Isaac and he looked a little more pathetic than he had when he had shot him that threatening glance downstairs. His breathing had become very heavy and Isaac thought he would collapse. He managed to steady himself and sat down on the chair. Isaac went to fetch a few of his clean clothes and placed them on the floor besides the bath. By the time he has come back the man had undressed and was now sitting in the bath. Isaac could see a multitude of wounds all over his back. They looked like knife slashes cutting into his pale skin. What had happened to this man?

Isaac left him to bathe and went downstairs to call the coast guard. He wanted this man out of the lighthouse as quickly as possible. He didn't trust him.
He tried the dial but only got static. Strange! He tried again and turned the dial all the way over then back again. There was nothing, not a peep from anywhere. He didn't like this. He checked the radio and everything was connected the way it should have been. He looked out of the window and could see clouds massing on the horizon. The heavy purple black clouds moved quickly towards the lighthouse as lightning cracked across the sky. A barrage of lightning flashes lit the sky and took over from the sunlight which had been totally obliterated by the storm clouds. The sky was covered with the slate clouds which seem to come in from every direction to converge on the lighthouse. The Sun was blocked out but no rain came just lightning spitting out of the dark blanket which hung heavy in the sky.
Isaac stepped out of the door and was met by a stifling heat. The atmosphere was so think he was beginning to have great difficulty in just breathing. A sharp crackle filled the air and he could feel the electricity running around the environment. Looking up, he could see lights in the sky. Lightning ran through the clouds illuminating them from within. The trapped electricity threatened to burst forth and destroy the sky, sea and land. The oppressive air clung to Isaac's clothing suffocating the life out of him. He stumbled back into the lighthouse and shut the door behind him.

As he turned, the man stood there naked before him. His mouth was opened as wide as it could go without splitting his cheeks. His tongue rattled violently between his teeth waiting for a scream to break the silence inside the room. His muscles were all taught throughout his badly deformed body. Isaac thought that a bolt of lightning had shot through his skull and was frying him from inside out. His convulsions continued and Isaac stepped away. The man came toward him with arms stretched out wide. Before he could reach Isaac, his eyes and mouth closed and his body went limp though he didn't fall. He just stood there with his head bowed down to his chest and his arms hanging loose by his sides. Scratches covered his arms and legs. They looked self inflicted. Old pink lines were etched into his forearms. They had stretched with his skin over time and some had turned his flesh white. The lank wet hair dripped from his head and beard onto the floor and had formed a small puddle where he stood. Isaac held his breath not wanting to move. This hideous statue looked like the limp puppet he had seen in his dreams. All of a sudden, it went pitch black. It was only eight o'clock in the morning although it looked like midnight. He could just make out the shape in front of him swaying side to side. Its arms now swung loosely in time with his torso. Isaac backed away as his eyes started to become accustomed to the darkness. The marionette in front of him lifted his head and let out a deathly scream. High pitched and piercing the noise rattled around the room with deafening volume. It ended as soon as it had begun and the black shape fell to the floor.

Isaac felt for the door handle behind him and pushed it down. His back pushed against it and he fell out onto the path. As he struggled to his feet, he looked up at the lighthouse and saw an orange glow emanating from the lantern room. White light ribbons danced around the tower going up and down the full height of the lighthouse. The whole building was bathed in white light and topped by a glowing orange radiance. He looked inside and couldn't see if the man was still there or not.

He turned and looked out to sea. It was as still as could be. Not a ripple broke the surface nor a wave could be seen. The seabirds had fallen silent and the sky boiled with the faint sound of thunder. Lights flashed through them and then stopped.

All around him was deathly silent.

CHAPTER EIGHT

The start of it all

No rest for the weary

To unburden the toil

A stranger draws near

Help will come in time

Hope is all that is left

No more one man can do

To shed the burden of the past

Total silence. Snow began to fall gently on the rocks and the sea. A sudden wind whipped white sleet through the night air. Swirls of snow had replaced the grey fog. Still, damp air cut through the atmosphere and clung to Isaac's face and clothes. The shroud of white covered everything in sight. A polar population of icy waves cut through the night like wallowing ghosts trapped in the ice blue tip of each crest. Shards of sharp white rivulets of ice bit into Isaac's face as he drew his heavy coat tighter to his body. They seemed to worm there way through the layers of his clothes to find his bare skin to attack and to freeze him.

The white light still caressed the lighthouse and all but the radio was silent. It crackled to itself inside and the static played out its monotonous rhythm. It sounded like a sonar beep but deeper and more menacing.

The sky was lit with curious shapes and colours. Red, blue and yellow flashes streaked across the sky through the black clouds. A deep rumble shook the sky. Crackles of wild electricity charged the clouds and a fork of light joined sky and sea making the water boil and bubble where it struck.

Suddenly, Isaac heard a sound of creaking wet wood. He saw where the bolt had struck the water. He could see the water begin to boil two hundred yards from the lighthouse as something big finally broke through the surface. The dark something slowly lifted and tilted through the frothing water. The wind started to pick up, and the snow turned to rain, heavy and drenching.

Isaac ran back inside to try and get the generator working. He frantically ripped the door open and panicked. He couldn't see a thing but managed to feel inside the dark and grasped hold of the lever. The generator spluttered into life, and the lights went from dim to bright within a few moments. He ran up through this lighthouse, twisting through the iron staircase which followed the sweeping contours of his home. He flicked switches and pulled levers as he went, lighting up the whole building

When he reached the lantern room he could see that the lighthouse beam was stationery and pointing out to land. He grabbed hold of the whole structure and turned it one hundred and eighty degrees on its mercury base around so that the vast light illuminated the bay. As he looked out into the beam he could see a broken ship begin to rise slowly, twisting and contorting as it came. Decaying strands of seaweed accompanied the huge vessel as it creaked and bent into an unsightly black wreck. The seaweed looked like filthy knotted hair trying to pull the ship back down to the depths. The more the seaweed pulled the more the ship began to break free. Black and sinewy, the seaweed looked like tough muscled arms gripping tightly to their prized possession. The struggle ended as the enormous ship lurched forward, ripped free from the grasp of the deep and fell heavily into the waiting sea.

It sat there, exhausted and derelict bathed in the light from Isaac's lantern. For what seemed like an eternity it sat there gaining strength before it made its next move. The sea started to swirl and thrash again. Another black tip rose out of the ocean skyward. A smaller vessel lifted itself out of the mire. Wood groaned and complained as it fought with the powers of the depths for freedom. Slowly, it began to liberate itself and finally sat in front of its big brother. The sea calmed again and was left to heal its wounds from the violent onslaught of these two ancient brutes.

Isaac saw the scene before him. His mind races along with his heart. He didn't want to take his eyes off the ships. Their broken hulls were sitting motionless on the ocean's surface. Isaac slowly made his way through the lighthouse. As he passed the bath he noticed a black slimy oil-like substance filled it. He quickly checked underneath his bed for the discarded coats but found nothing there. His bedroom looked skewed and alien to his eyes. The bed was stood on it end, trapped between the floor and ceiling. Its bed clothes were stained black and red as though they had been discarded from a slaughter house. His chair and wardrobe were mangled together, entwined in a lover's embrace. The chair legs bent and wrapped around the wardrobes bulk seemed to pulsate and breathe. Groaning noises came from the room as the ceiling began to crack. Isaac rushed for the steps as pieces of plaster freed themselves from the ceiling and crashed down onto the wooden floor. The chest of drawers began to walk slowly towards him. The three pictures had been nailed through the glass onto the front drawers of the piece of furniture. Each picture was enlarged to four times its original size. Blood red tears splattered each of the pictures. The figures howled and screamed his name. Crying, screaming, and wailing. Pain and torture filled their voices.

"Isaac! Bastard!" they yelled. He could see the faces of his parents his ex wife and he himself contorting their features with anguish and pain. Steam's mutilated body was depicted on the third with black slime and seaweed spewing out from his slit stomach. Isaac recoiled in revulsion.

He reached the ground floor where he found no sign of his erstwhile guest. Cracks appeared in the wall of lighthouse as black slug-like creatures squirmed their way through to the warmth inside. The door was wide open and he stepped out into the gloom.

An eerie silence met him. The ships sat there. Waiting. He held his binoculars to his eyes and searched the ships decks. He saw that everything was destroyed. Great holes covered their sides and broken wood was scattered about their decks. The larger ships looked menacing as it stood silently in the murky water. The rain and snow had subsided now as he stood on the drenched rocks. A chilling feeling ran through his whole body as he surveyed the desolation that he saw. The white aura still clung to the lighthouse behind him. A load crack made him jump and he almost lost his footing. He steadied himself and lowered the binoculars. Another loud snap shot through the air. He could see the ships moving now. As they did he could make out the wood folding and reshaping itself. The great holes began to restore themselves and wood and metal bent around its flanks. As the ship picked up speed, they transformed into what they should had been. Two huge funnels twisted out of the wreckage of the larger vessel and began to reform into the metal chimneys they had once been. Smoke began to rise out of them and Isaac could hear a deep thrum from its renewed engines. The small ship manifested itself into a cargo vessel of some size. Its proud form shimmied and shook as it made its way towards the lighthouse.

Then the thunder came. Lashing rain and flashing lightning joined in and tore the sky apart. Black, purple and red shadows covered the heavens as yellow licks of light sped over them. Giant rolling clouds fought each other, clashing sending sparks and lightning as they collided. The ships below craved for freedom and were beaten down by the relentless rain. A loud crack and a flash electrified the air around him. A rumble and a crash followed behind him over towards land. He charged around to the west side of the lighthouse to see the black rock face shuttering down into the sea. A huge slab of cliff slid down into the water creating a wave ten feet high riding out to meet the oncoming weather. Boulders followed by mud and vegetation tumbled down the cliff side accelerating towards the rocky foot of the cliffs. The roar of the water speed out to sea. Enormous waves came in droves from the east and attacked the new land formed wave. They hit and water shot fifty feet high. The shower of water mingled with the rain and fogged out the view.

Isaac was standing, watching the scene. He didn't know which way to look as he was in the middle of a hurricane. The wind was trying to make him release his grip but it only made him more determined to hang on. He clung onto the rail for his life. A scream and a frightening whistling sound rang out from the ruined rocks. He could see hundreds or even thousands of black birds flying out of the destroyed cliff, blocking out even the monumental clouds with their blackness. They came towards the lighthouse in an unyielding force. Their chatter they brought was hi-pitched screams. Then Isaac realised that these black birds had leathery wings. Bats! Huge venomous flying rodents. Each one must have had a wingspan over almost three feet. As they came, he tried run into the shelter of the lighthouse. He managed it just in time as they all flew around the lighthouse through the white light and screeched as they touched it. Fire engulfed the tower as the bats burst into flames. Hundreds of them burned and fell into the sea boiling it with their touch. The bats fell in hoards into the fierce waves. The light emitted by the lighthouse had acted as some protective shield against the ghastly creatures. Those that had avoided the light flew directly towards the ships. Isaac could still see hundreds upon hundreds of them stream through the black rain illuminated be the constant lightning flashes and the beam from the lighthouse. It looked like a black and white horror movie from the twenties as the light stuttered in the sky. Rapid lightning flashes gave the scene an even more archaic tone. They converged into an arrow shape and struck the ships. Each hit the wooden carcasses like darts embedding themselves deep into the ancient crafts innards. Splinters of wood flew into the air like wood shavings being expelled from a wood chipper. Sawdust mixed with the rain and was beaten down into the frenzy below. He could see that the ships were not halted by this assault as they raised high in the waves and continued on their way. The damage that the bats had done was quickly repaired as the broken wood reformed into its original shape. Whatever evil had been sent to stop the ships had failed.

As he watched, Isaac could see splashing in the water around the rocks of the lighthouse. The crews of the ships wanted to be reunited with the two ships. Their lifeless bodies rose to the surface in small clusters. Clothes, ravaged by the deep hung off the corpses' bodies like flaps of skin torn away from the meat and bones. Dead eyes stared into the black sky which looked straight back into them with guilt and horror. The dead should stay dead. The sea had claimed them and wasn't going to make it easy. Heavy rain fell from the storm clouds above and fought with the sea. The storm intensified and drove wave after wave over the broken bodies, subjecting them to the same punishment which had been bestowed upon them a century ago.

These were the ships which had sunk here back in 1870. Were they coming back to punish their murderer's blood line for their loss?

As the fog horn blasted its powerful voice across the bay, it seemed to give strength to the ships, their crew and passengers. Eerie screams filled the air, vying for dominance above the sound of the thunder. Bodies left the ocean, as though shot from a catapult, back toward the ships twisted railings. The vessels captured the flailing bodies with ease and let them rest on the decks. Bodies flinched and sat upright. Hundreds of figures now covered the deck of the Livingstone. Eyes still closed, one by one, they felt for good a hold in the encompassing storm and stood proud on the decks.

The storm seemed to ease, as the final bodies found their place on the vessels. With his binoculars clamped to his unbelieving eyes, Isaac stared at the deck of the steamship and could see the crew stood firmly holding the railings. As he slowly scanned the crew, he could now see that their eyes we're open, yellow, searching dreadful eyes. One crew member, bedecked in captain's clothing, looked directly at Isaac and into his soul.

"Isaac," a voice in his head said. The voice came again. "Isaac."

The ancient seaman told Isaac a story of long, long ago. Of another named Isaac who manned the old lighthouse on which the Thornside now stood. Of his Great Grandfather. Of a man who took no responsibility for anything, though the sinking of the two vessels sat upon his shoulder and his alone.

On the night of December the third, 1870 the Crantock had set sail from Aberdeen to carry its cargo to Rotterdam. The cruise liner Livingstone, sailed the same waters in a terrible storm.

A passenger on the liner had relieved many of them their belongings when the chaos of the storm began. Wallets, watches and jewellery were quickly stuffed into the pockets of coats he had also stolen. More coats, more pockets, more places to stash his contraband. He slashed and cut his victims, leaving them bleeding.

As the Livingstone began to list and sink, he made his way to the life-boats guarded by two sailors to each boat. As he approached, the sailors shouted, "Woman and children only." The muzzle of the rifle flashed in the night and the first sailor fell with the skull missing from his forehead. The other sailor ran, but was hit by the second shot, planted in his back. The thief dropped the weapon and ran for the lifeboat.

The thief made his way onto the boat, just as the ship leaned to the portside. The boat hit the water and the force released its shackles. The thief grabbed the remaining oar, and began to row with all that his strength could muster. Clear of the ship, the waves did their best to remove the charlatan from the tiny sanctuary. The thief landed his small craft on the rocks of the nearby lighthouse.

The lighthouse was home to a man who had been sanctioned with the duty to light the beacon and to keep safe the waters travellers. That night, he had readied himself for the storm which was approaching fast. He knew how bad the weather could get and he had no desire to see another unfortunate vessel introduced to the dangers rocks of the Thornwick bay. As the storm hit, Isaac of 1870 readied himself to climb the steps up to the lantern room. He had been to the lantern room to ignite the flame. Someone got in his way that night and he failed to do his duty. He had a visitor that night. Two hundred and fifty four men, women and children died that night. Only one would survive.

Isaac Shepherd was shocked to hear such a noise when the thief banged on his door. Isaac opened the door and was faced with the thief. He had black sores covering his face and his grey hair hung in wet rat-tails over his features. He pushed his way in threatening Isaac. Death filled his eyes as he staggered toward Isaac. He couldn't fight back as he was unprepared for the attack. The thief took a good hold of Isaac and threw him to the floor. He smashed into the barrels of whale oil used for lighting the flame and lay spread-eagled on the floor. The liquid spread beneath Isaac as he lay there defenceless.

"Keeper", he hissed through broken teeth. Foul, vile breath spewed forth from his black mouth. He lunged forward. The knife shone brightly in the night as it slashed and cut at Isaac's body. It was thrust deeply into his neck and blood flowed from the gaping wound over the hand of the thief. Isaac tried to speak but blood bubbled in his throat as he drew in breath. Breath that he couldn't hold as the air mixed with the blood and all he could manage was a gargled groan. The thief stood over him as life ebbed away with the blood and the oil.

In all the chaos outside and no-one left to vouch for him, he took hold of the ancestor of Isaac and dragged him to the door and threw his lifeless body into the lifeboat. The oil had soaked through Isaac's dying body and as he bent down to look into his pale face, the thief opened the lighter. He flicked it alight and touched the oil soaked body lying on the rocks. The flames engulfed the lighthouse keeper as the thief watched on. Isaac screamed and convulsed with the pain as the thief laughed pushed the boat out to sea then turned his back on him. He leaned against the lighthouse wall and took out a cigarette case. He took out one of the five remaining cigarettes and lit it.

The thief then stole something new: the lighthouse keeper's identity. They were a similar build and both had grey hair and at a distance they could pass as brothers. The thief hacked at his own hair to get it shorter and more like his victim. He knew nothing about running a lighthouse and had slept there and ate what food remained. He drank the last of the rum and had started on Isaac's wine and beer supply. In a drunken stupor, he attempted to light the flame of the lantern. Swigging from the bottle he threw in a rag soaked in kerosene. The lantern took the light and roared into life. The thief didn't think it would take light so quickly and was taken aback by the furious heat. He fumbled with the door hatch and could not open it. Anger made him throw the bottle at the flame which exploded showering him with fire. He thrashed and yelled but to no avail. His hair set alight as he tried to put it out. His clothes and hair now burnt bright orange in the room.

When the full horror of the captain's story had finished, Isaac saw the ragged coats swirl through the storms wind. Chalk-like stones and sticks formed into a grotesque skeleton, and seaweed and sand clung to the bones. Black shiny stones shot into the eye sockets and the coats wrapped themselves around the hideous form. It looked directly at Isaac and opened its mouth to scream. Arms that were out-stretched to the side of its body slowly wrapped themselves around the torso and hugged tightly. Only a croak at first until the thief drew sea air into its fetid lungs, and after a hundred years, screamed. The banshee screech cut through the air like a sword and all but its voice could be heard. The storm retreated and the rain ceased. The thief lurched forward to grab at Isaac with terrible roar. Isaac's reactions were at a heightened state and he deftly dodged the lunge and struck the thief on the back with both fists as he passed him by. The thief stumbled and Isaac quickly kicked at his back. The madman lost his footing and sprawled across the floor. As quick as the lightning that was beginning again and creating chaos outside, Isaac stepped forward and grabbed at the fire axe next to the door. The thief turned to see Isaac standing over him ready to strike. The old thief cackled and laughed in Isaac's face as the axe came down with a crunch through his skull. Isaac stepped back and let the fiend thrash about on the blood soaked floor still with the axe embedded into its evil head.

"Death to you, old man," screeched the thief as it finally fell forward, dead.

"Isaac." That voice again. Isaac looked across at the seaman. The captain's eyes now glowed in the night and all the ships lights shone brilliantly in the dark. Isaac heard shuffling behind him and there stood the thief. The axe had gone and so had the wound. The transparent ghost of the thief looked over to his tormentor on the ship and then back at Isaac. As Isaac watched, the thief was struck by a black grappling hook and began to be hauled jerkily through the rain toward the ship. Isaac absentmindedly rubbed at the white scar on his hand.

Isaac fetched his binoculars in time to see the thief land on the deck of the ship. As he landed, two sailors came forward to put him in irons and chains. One sailor had no forehead, whereas the other had a gaping hole in his back. As Isaac watched, the sailors smiled a grim smile. They tied the evil lying thief to the ships mast and ripped away his coats and shirt. Another man stepped forward holding a whip. The cat-o-nine-tails was drawn back and then with a quick snap struck the bare back of the thief. Isaac could hear his screams through the night. The storm and rain stopped to allow the punishment to commence. Again and again the whip cracked through the air like lightning. As each strike connected a lightning flash accompanied it. The thief slumped under the bite of the vicious whip. The thief was taken away as the captain saluted Isaac.

Laughter and band music sifted through the air from the ship as the cargo ship sailed on and out to sea to deliver it's precious wares. The smoke filed behind the large ship as it too got under way after a one hundred year rest. As he watched, both the ship and the cargo vessel turned to mist on the sea.

As Isaac watched the ships, he felt a relief. All these months in fear of what was happening to him it was now that he began to understand. He thought that his brain was beginning to become unhinged. His dreams had been about the thief and his crimes that were due to be punished. He had started to think that his Great Grandfather had been responsible for everything that had happened one hundred years ago. The thief had already got to the lighthouse before the lantern could be lighted. Isaac Shepherd would have managed to get the lantern alight had the thief not arrived from the sea. He had been murdered and the thief had left the ships to crash and to be destroyed in the ensuing storm. The thief allowed so many deaths and the blood was on his hands. It had always been that way but the records showed that it was his ancestor who had been blamed for the tragedy.

Isaac now knew the truth but he was powerless to let the world know what had happened. Who would believe that the captain of a ship which had sunk a hundred years previously had told him what had happened?

The weather was starting to improve now and the rain had subsided. The waves lapped gently over the rocks. Isaac noticed that something has washed up onto them and he tentatively walked around to find a body. With everything he had happened to him he now wondered what else was coming his way. He pulled the lifeless body up and onto the path. The clothing of the RNLI lifeboat made him realise that he was holding onto the body of George Meade. Unlike the other five bodies that had been washed up months ago, George's body was not burnt and appeared to be undamaged. There was no sign of rigour mortis as Isaac looped his arms underneath

George's and dragged him back into the lighthouse. He sat him in the chair. He stared down at the man whom he had spoken to on so many occasions over the years but had never met. How ironic to see him for the first time like this, although, something felt wrong. Even though the body had been in the water since the accident, it was warm. Isaac lifted George's right arm and felt his wrist with his forefinger. There was a faint pulse. George was alive. How could that be? Quickly, Isaac fetched blankets and wrapped them tightly around George's body. He brought with him a glass of water and raised it up to George's lips. His body jerked and he spluttered. Slowly, he opened his eyes.

"What happened?" he coughed.

Isaac held the glass to his mouth and George drank deeply.

"George, it's Isaac. How do you feel?"

"Not good. My chest hurts."

"Do you remember anything?"

George looked around the room. "Isaac?" then his eyes closed again.

Isaac couldn't quite believe what he was seeing. The boat had exploded and the coastguard had found five badly burnt bodies. George had not been recovered and it was believed that his body would never been found. Yet, here he was, alive and well, breathing sat in the armchair in front of him.

"A gift," said a voice in his head. "We've given him back to you as a gift."

The captain's voice spoke deep inside his body.

Isaac heard an explosion and rushed outside. He felt the heat from the flames now shooting from the lantern room. As glass shattered around him he could see a figure flailing around in the flames, screaming as the hot molten lead fell from the roof of the lantern room. Was this how the thief had died back in 1870?

Isaac ran back into the lighthouse and up the steps until he reached the watch room. The hatch was blackened with smoke billowing through the scorched wood. Looking around him, he found wet coats slumped in a corner. Grabbing them quickly, Isaac threw them over his head and leapt up the ladder. He burst through the door to find no no-one there.

He frantically looked around the lantern room for any sign of the figure he had seen but the room was empty. The framework and the glass were in a mess. He felt sick to his stomach and the room began to swirl around him. He tried to grab at anything that would keep him from falling but his hands grasped at air. Total fatigue took over his body and he collapsed to the floor, banged his forehead on the window and lost consciousness.

The black clouds retreated and a pale yellow sun struggled to break through the white clouds which were left behind. As the birds began to gather in the sky, silver rain fell from the new virgin clouds to cleanse the rocks and the lighthouse and to rid the place of the foul stench and the filth. The seabirds flew down to search the clear pools nestled between the huge rocks surrounding the base of the lighthouse. Sunlight danced in the shallow waters as gulls splashed in search of stray fish. Shells, housing limpets, hid low in the water to escape the onslaught of the squawking predators. Sparkling spray from the waves shimmered in the new day sunshine creating rainbows from every drop. The shiny jewels of light gave the rocks a delicate web-like covering. A million precious gems gleamed there awaiting eager treasure hunters to come and sweep them into their thankful arms. Only the seagulls came to claim their prizes in the more familiar shape of silver fish washed up onto the rocks and into the pools after failing to return to the safety of the sea water and to its depths. Hungry beaks clashed with rock as they snapped and cawed in their pursuit; easy pickings for ravenous birds. The remnants of the storm left cool brisk winds to clear the way for better weather. The birds left with the oncoming wind as the rocks had been picked bare of the bounteous morsels. A familiar little bird landed on the distressed path and looked about for an easy meal. Bill hopped slowly along the path towards the broken door. He could no longer see that tall grey shape which would give him his breakfast. His head flitted from left to right, then he looked up towards the lamp of the lighthouse and took off. He flew over the lighthouse, sang a little song then flew back to the cliffs.

A clear bright rainbow draped itself across the sky to announce the end of the storm. Its magnificent colours seemed amplified against the still steel grey clouds of the departing force which had torn the sky open with lightning and fire. A new day beckoned and some hope seemed to be closing in from the far horizon.

The shower became lighter, as though the sky had exhausted it's tears. Those tears rained down for those who had perished one hundred years ago.
Tears for Isaac?

Isaac lay there for two days. As daylight came he blinked at the glare and his head hurt. He could hear a very faint sound coming from downstairs and he tried to stand and call for help. His voice broke as he yelled. Panic ran through his body.

Peter sailed up to the lighthouse to see a disaster zone. The lighthouse had been battered from the top of the lantern to the base on the rocks below. He saw the door broken on its hinges and it listed sickeningly inwards. Looking up at the lighthouse he could see burn marks covering the whole tower. The red sash that surrounded the lighthouse tower looked as though it had begun to drip down through the white paint of the lighthouse. Dead birds and fish littered the rocks but there was no sign of his friend. The glass in the lantern room was smashed and sharp teeth protruded from the frames. The light itself was missing.

He moved closer to the lighthouse and brought his boat around the back to the small jetty. He quickly secured the boat and leapt onto the rocks. He ran around to the door and burst in. "Isaac!" he shouted.

As soon as he entered the lighthouse, he saw George sat in the chair. His heart stopped. He could see George's chest rise and lower as he took in deep breaths. What had gone on here? The lighthouse was in a real mess yet he finds his old friend sat sleeping in Isaac's chair.

"Isaac!" he shouted again. Nothing. Debris was strewn around the room and it looked like a tornado had swept through the whole place. Isaac's paintings were ripped and torn. His furniture was broken and trashed. He looked down at George and knelt down by him. He gently touched his arm and George's head moved around. His eyes opened and look straight at Peter.

"Peter?"

"I'm here. What's going on?"

"No idea. Isaac wrapped me up here."

"This is amazing. Do you remember anything at all?"

George swallowed deeply and rubbed him neck.

"I remember being on my boat then a flash. There was a searing heat then nothing."

"Where's Isaac?"

"I don't know."

Peter shouted again.

Peter frantically searched the room and opened the door to the larder and checked behind the overturned furniture. He looked up at the steps and charged onwards. Some of the steps were missing, broken or bent. He managed to scale them and arrived in the bedroom area. The bed was in disarray. Blankets and pillows were tattered and blowing from the wind coming in through the shattered window. Again he shouted for Isaac. No reply came. He checked the small bathroom and found it destroyed. The silver mirror lay shattered in the sink. The watch room was above him. He climbed the steps and saw the supply boxes torn and split. Their content spilled out over the floor, but there was no sign of Isaac here. The hatch above him was twisted and broken. He could not get it open.

He opened the outer door and ran up the twenty steps to the lantern room. He climbed over the broken door and found Isaac lying in a heap on the floor. Blood covered his head and Peter gasped at the sight. Isaac's body was in a mess. As he moved closer to him, he could see that he had coats wrapped around his body. They had obviously kept him warm but had they kept him alive? Peter bent down and placed his hand on his old friends shoulder and gently moved him over. Isaac grunted and looked up into the relieved face of Peter. Fear and shock covered his face as he looked into Peter's damp eyes.

"Isaac. Come on, Isaac stay with me. Isaac, Isaac! My God, are you okay?"

Isaac managed to raise a smile then drifted off again into a deep sleep.

CHAPTER NINE

Souls are now free

To be what they be

A price to take heed

For the strongest there is

For five score years

And all of their fears

Just one pays the deed

And lays the life which was his

For almost thirty years, Isaac had manned the Thornside Lighthouse. As times
changed and technology brought in new innovative ways of improving automation, it
came to the point where a lighthouse no longer needed to have a keeper anymore. All
controls could be dealt with at Trinity House. It was now 1986 and Isaac was relieved
of his duties. He knew it was coming and at sixty nine years of age it was time for him
to relax. After all those years, the terrible events of sixteen years ago were still alive
in his memory. He'd survived that experience but not without any repercussions. His
health had suffered both mentally and physically. The scar across his forehead would
never go although the emotional scars even ran deeper. His life had not been without
its heartache. He had lost his wife twice. He saw her taken away by that rocker then
Jake had ended her life. Isaac felt no comfort that Jake had also taken his own

miserable life as well. But all that was a long time ago and Isaac now just wanted to rest. Years of heartache lay behind him and a peaceful and relaxing life lay ahead.

As Isaac was checking through the lighthouse and packing the last of his belongings, he heard a boat arrive. It was Peter. His friend had aged but his kindly eyes still twinkled.

"Ahoy there you old seadog," a familiar voice shouted.

Isaac moved to the door as quickly as his old legs would allow and saw his dear old friend waving as he approached.

"Peter," Isaac waved. This man had saved him in more ways than one. Isaac would be moving in with Peter and his lovely wife, Sally. He didn't know what he would do when he was told that he would have to leave the lighthouse, but Peter came up with the goods as he always had done. They had plenty of room in their house and they said they would be honoured if he saw out his days with them.

Peter pulled the boat into the little jetty and threw the rope to Isaac to tie around the mooring hook. He hadn't noticed the other man standing behind Peter.

"Isaac, I've brought a friend with me," he said nodding toward the tall man.

Someone from Trinity House come to see me off, thought Isaac. His pension had all been agreed and they had looked after him very well. His service had been exemplary according to the company.

The other man stepped off the boat and stood looking at Isaac.

"Can we go inside?" he said to Isaac. He was smartly dressed and very polite. Maybe I'll be getting a gold watch from this company man, he thought to himself.

"Please sit yourself down young man." Isaac offered him a seat.

Peter stood outside looking at his boat. Isaac looked over and watched his friend rearrange some boxes and bags.

"Mr. Shepherd," the man said, "There's something I need to tell you. My name is Andrew."

"I'm very pleased to meet you, Andrew."

"And I'm your son."

Isaac sat there wanting to say something but nothing came out.

"I'm sorry," he finally managed to say. "You're my son?"

"I know it's not easy to hear, but please let me try to explain."

"Peter!" Isaac shouted now getting agitated.

Peter appeared at the door. "It's alright, Isaac. Listen to what he has to say."

Isaac looked at the man and saw a familiar look in his eyes. Those grey blue calming eyes he had seen in the mirror for almost seventy years.

Andrew reached out to hold his hand. Isaac flinched but sat still as this stranger took hold of him. This man exuded a warmth and charm about him. Isaac listened to what he had to say.

"I was born in 1940, during the war. My mother was young and on her own after you'd left for the Navy. Her parents thought it best that I was sent out into the country where it would be safer. I was nothing but a baby and was sent out as a refugee to Cornwall with a neighbour's son and daughter. The family who looked after me also took in two other children. Jeremy and Susan were only eight and ten and I was sent along as their baby brother. As I grew up, life was wonderful and fun living with my new family. By the time the war had ended, I was still only five years old and the family who had taken me in wrote to my mother to let her know that I was safe and ready to return home. My mother had got used to not having me around and had started to make arrangements for you to come home to her. She wanted that time with you and didn't want anything to come between you."

Isaac felt that Alice had tried to shield her son from the truth. She didn't want Isaac to come back from the war. Andrew continued.

"She wrote back to the family and asked them to look after me saying that her husband had died during the war and she didn't think that she'd be able to look after a five year old boy. I had become my foster parent's son. I had been with them from being a baby and believed that they were my parents. Jeremy and Susan had to leave to go back to their own families and I was devastated. We were three small children from three very different families. I didn't understand. Roger and Jill, my new family cared for me and put me through schooling. We moved to Truro a few years later where Roger's had to go for his job. It was a beautiful place."

Isaac sat and listened. He couldn't really believe what was happening here.

Andrew went on.

"One my sixteenth Birthday, my foster parents had decided that I should know the truth and told me about my mother. It took me a while to come to terms with being abandoned and I couldn't understand why it had happened. I was angry and frustrated and wanted to see my mother. I didn't have her address as she had moved since the war. I now know that you had moved to the Bradford area together but I wanted to see her again."

Andrew looked into his father's eyes.

"I finally managed to track her down and sent her a letter. She agreed to meet me and came with Jake. I didn't know who he was. He didn't seem to be much older than I was at the time. This was in 1962 and I was twenty two years old by then. A year later she died in a car crash. At her funeral, I stood with my Grandparents and my girlfriend, Barbara. Grandma had been in a car accident and couldn't walk or really understand anything anymore. I saw you standing over near the trees. I mentioned this to my Granddad. He was old and caring for my Grandma then and had a lot to think about. He told me that you weren't killed in the war. I was angry and confused at being lied to yet again. My whole life had been a lie and I was only catching up with my family years later. I had not known my real mother for the first eighteen years of my life and then I found out about you. Barbara stood by me and listened to my problems. A few years later, Grandma died and Granddad followed soon after. I'd lost all my real family but I knew that you were out there."

Isaac stopped him there.

"I never knew about you Andrew. Alice must have got pregnant very quickly before I went to war. There was never any talk about you. I didn't know you even existed."

"I know. I don't blame you for anything."

Peter came in and quietly went through to the kitchen and boiled some water. He brought three mugs of tea over, settled two of them down and went back outside into the sunshine. Isaac could see Peter looking out to sea.

"How did you find me?"

"Just before my Granddad died, he told me that you had moved to the coast after he let you go from the factory. He knew nothing about your whereabouts other than that. I found out where you were about fifteen years ago. I read about the lighthouse in the paper and saw your name. There had been an accident and the lighthouse had to be closed down for repairs?"

"Yes," said Isaac, "the lighthouse was in need of some repair."

Peter turned and looked through the door and winked at Isaac. Isaac cracked a smile.

"Yes, there was an incident. Carry on, please," Isaac squeezed his son's hand.

Andrew looked down at the old man's hand and gently squeezed back. This was going better than he thought.

"I wanted to contact you then, but Barbara thought it would be better to let things calm down first."

"So, are you still with Barbara?" Isaac asked smiling.

"Barbara has been my wife now for twenty years."

"Children?" Isaac asked eagerly.

"Two; a girl and a boy. Chris is eighteen now and at University. I have a photo of him here in my wallet."

He brought out a Polaroid picture of a handsome young man with fair hair.

"And your daughter?"

"Alice," said Andrew.

Peter walked through the door with a beautiful petite young woman.

"Alice, this is your Grandfather."

Isaac eyes welled up.

"Hello," she said. Isaac stood up and held his arms out to her.

She hugged him. "We have you now and we won't let go," she said kissing him gently on his cheek.

Isaac let all of his emotions out. His tears were at last for joy as his son joined them. The three of them held each other and Isaac sobbed uncontrollably.

Peter walked back out of the door. He looked about him, taking in the scenery and the view. Seagulls began to swoop over head and call to their friends. The new fog horn had been installed two months ago and the remote control units placed in the lighthouse. The full refurbishment of Thornwick lighthouse could take place now that Isaac was leaving. Peter knew it was hard for his old friend to leave, but knew that the time had come for him to move on. Since the events sixteen years ago, Peter and Isaac's friendship had grown even more. He and Sally had visited the lighthouse many times over the years and he had seen his old friend get older and older. He was almost fifty years old himself, but Isaac could still run rings around him. Isaac was a strong man even at sixty nine and had no real problems with running the lighthouse but it was time to go.

He walked back through the door to see the family reunited.

"Dad," Andrew said. "Peter had kindly offered you the opportunity to go and live with him and Sally. I'd like to offer you an alternative. Come and live with us, we have the room."

"I don't know what to say."

"Come and visit, spend some time with us and see how you feel. We have a large house in a small village in North Yorkshire. We have an extension where you could live. It has its own bedroom, kitchen and living room. We used it for Chris before he moved out. We'd have to get rid of his posters. I can't see you looking up at Iron Maiden posters strewn around the room".

Isaac looked over to Peter. Peter nodded. "The choice is yours, old friend."

Isaac took out the silver pocket watch and gave it a quick wind.

"Time to go," he said.

Two months later, Isaac sat sipping lemonade in the garden. Andrew's house was a beautiful old Victorian dwelling which had been lovingly decorated. Cooling fans hung down from the high ceilings in the living room, dining room and the large conservatory. Several painting hung in prime places throughout the house. Isaac's pictures adorned the walls in the dining room and one was placed at the top of the staircase. Andrew too, was a keen artist and had displayed many of his art work in installations in various museums and galleries across the country.

Alice sat next to him. They had become inseparable since they met only nine short weeks ago. He looked down at her swelling tummy. Alice rubbed it absentmindedly. She was now three months pregnant and her fiancé was talking with Peter and Andrew. Peter laughed and tendered the barbeque. Sausages and steak spat and sizzled. Chicken, peppers and onion kebabs sat at their side. Bowls of fresh salad sat on the garden table. Water glistened on the red ripe tomatoes. Isaac's new found family stood or sat around soaking up the sun and drinking wine and beer. He had his son and daughter in law, two wonderful grandchildren and had become firm friends with Jeremy and Susan, the two children that his son had spent the early years of his life with in Cornwall. They laughed and played with their own children, Archie and Arthur. Andrew seemed to be quite the master of tracking people down it appeared.

Barbara called out, "Alice, bring your Grandfather over to the barbeque."
"Be there in a minute!" she shouted back.
"Come on, let's get some food." She held his hand and helped him to his feet. Since he had left the lighthouse, he had become weaker but happier. Not having to run up and down the steps or lift the heavy supply bags that Peter would bring had softened his muscles.

Alice lightly stroked the beautiful necklace her grandfather had given her. The jewels shone in the afternoon sun and diamond crystals split the light into a million shards of sumptuous light. She smiled at him. He choked at her looks. She had her grandmother's eyes and mouth. He looked up into Alice's face and saw his wife smiling back at him. He took her hand and made their way to the decking and the barbeque where his family now stood.

They walked past the model which sat in the centre of the garden. Light reflected off the shiny little windows and the white and red tower gleamed bright in the sunlight. Isaac let his hand brush its roof as he walked passed.

EPILOGUE

In Reality...

Third December, 1870

The thief ran up to the lantern room and doused the flames, extinguishing the only light for the ships out in the bay. He watched the waves take control of the vessels and saw how quickly they became lost in their own battle of survival. Wave after wave crashed into the smaller ship, twisting it round and round and out of control. Bodies were being tossed overboard and a fire broke out on the deck as a fuel barrel ignited. A huge shot of fire spouted up into the black rain just as it rammed into the ship. Broken wood splintered and split. The ship listed and broke in two. The lights all went out and it began to sink. As he started to descend the steps a stray spark taken up from the iron cradle of the lantern, caught the thief's hair. Screaming and shouting, he clutched his head in his hands and flames covered his head. The thief ran screaming down the steps, tears streaming down his scorched face. He reached the ground floor and jumped out through the front door and into the rain. Grey smoke rose from his head as he plunged his damaged face into the seawater. He lay still with his head submerged until the stinging began to subside. He pushed himself up and looked out at the ships and gave an almighty victorious roar.

The thief was badly burnt during the fire. His blackened face was almost unrecognisable even to himself. He knew that he had to move quickly. He could see that the two vessels had collided and were sinking fast. He could hear the screaming from the dying as they were sucked down into the depths by the huge ship. He had killed the lighthouse keeper and he turned his attention to the battered body of Isaac Shepherd. Looking down at the dead keeper an idea began to form. They were the same build and approximate age. He went to the sink in the kitchen and began to wash his face to try and cool his burns. He stripped Isaac's body and then removed his own tattered clothes. Climbing into the clothes of the lighthouse keeper he thought how he could dispose of the blackened corpse. He dragged Isaac's body out into the pouring rain and retrieved the lifeboat he had used and placed him inside. Pushing the boat out into the sea he believed that, should the boat be found anyone would think that it was some unfortunate soul who had tried to escape from one of the ships.

Walking back inside, he slumped down into the old chair. A whiskey bottle lay discarded beneath the chair and he pulled off the top and drank deeply, stripping the flesh from his throat. He spat it out onto the floor, before taking another swig. He wiped his mouth and saw black burnt skin covering the back of his hand. He knew that he could pass as the former lighthouse keeper and maybe get something out of this. He lost consciousness and dropped the bottle to the floor.

He sat there for two days before a boat showed up at the lighthouse. The weather had improved sufficiently for anyone to venture out. As the crew members leapt off the boat, the thief began to stir. He was taken ashore and was met by Isaac Shepherd's wife. His throat had been burnt so badly that he could not talk. He kept his mouth closed and just looked up into the face of this woman. At the sight of his burned face and body, she burst into tears and threw herself onto him. She wept and thanked the Lord that her husband had been brought back to her. The thief smiled and again passed out from exhaustion and pain.

Five days later, the thief lay in bed with the wife of Isaac Shepherd as she gently rocked back and forth on his body. He knew that he was dying. His breathing had become laboured from the inhalation of the smoke from his burns just a few days before. He could feel his lungs getting tighter and shrivelling up inside. He had one last thing to do. As he thrust deeper into her, he planted the seed that would become Tobias Shepherd.

2012 Robert Pearson □ Dead Lullabies

Printed in Great Britain
by Amazon

21037913R00098